A Deadly December in Edgemont

Village of Edgemont, Volume 1

Della North

Published by Lynda French, 2023.

A DEADLY DECEMBER IN EDGEMONT

First edition. September 30, 2023.

Copyright © 2023 Della North.

ISBN: 978-1998074068

Written by Della North.

A heartfelt thank you to Darlene Hartung for her wonderful encouragement, it means a lot.

Chapter One

The body of missing teen Holly Lezinsky was found on December 19th, just two days before her fourteenth birthday. She'd been missing for one week and pregnant for eleven.

The discovery didn't affect Judith's plans for Christmas because she didn't have any, but she did have to rearrange the school's ruined holiday schedule. "Luckily there are only a few more days left, and the workload is light," she thought.

Although the news was sad Judith felt it was important that they learned the truth at last. It had been a very unsettling week for staff and students alike as everyone worried over Holly's whereabouts. She was a popular girl.

School Principal Patricia Johnson got the call from the police. They would be coming around later today or tomorrow with questions and to hold some interviews because it was a suspicious death. Well of course it was, the victim was just a child although Judith was quite sure Holly didn't see herself as such!

Pat answered the officer's call herself since Samira, the school secretary, was off sick with the flu. A nasty bug making the rounds had already affected staff and students. She called Judith and apologised for giving her the news over the phone but excused that claiming a pounding headache and a million things to do adding:

"I'll have to make an announcement but I'm hoping to get more information from the police first. Everyone's going to have so many questions. Ugh, I just can't think about it all right now."

Judith discovered that she wasn't shocked to hear the new, figuring she must have suspected that Holly was already dead. Holly did seem like the kind of girl to get into trouble. Unless it was suicide? How was she killed? Unfortunately, it wasn't a stretch to imagine Holly as a murder victim.

Judith did wonder "Am I being unfair to the girl?" but then an image of Holly in her school uniform came to mind: plaid skirt rolled up at the waist to shorten it, shirt unbuttoned to show the lace on her bra, and knee socks rolled down to her ankles to flash a lot of bare leg.

Holly Lezinsky was a brazen adolescent flaunting her new-found sexuality but the poor girl didn't deserve to die.

Of course, Judith felt terribly sorry for the girl's family. Holly was raised by a single mom and she was an only child, an upbringing similar to Judith's own. She started wondering about how her own mother would have coped in such a circumstance but forcefully slammed the door shut on such thoughts. The past was dead and gone. She had resolved a long time ago to move on.

Still, it seemed that somehow a death was made even worse when it happened so close to Christmas. Judith thought that the happiness of others would be unbearable to the bereaved. And then each successive anniversary would be another reminder.

"Well, it's not my concern. It's up to the police now," thought Judith. Opening the scheduling app on her laptop she forgot about the girl and got to work revising the plans for the next few days.

Chapter Two

She got back to work thinking "No more distractions, I definitely want to finish the Accounts Receivable today. I'm not going to let this delay me starting my holidays tomorrow," Judith decided. "I suppose that's selfish but honestly this girl's death is nothing to do with me."

Her phone buzzed with another internal call from the principal. Judith sighed. Pat Johnson came straight to the point saying:

"Judith, I hope you haven't booked anything because I can't let you go on vacation yet. I need you here. I could have managed on my own without my secretary but not with Holly's death as well. The phone is ringing non-stop. In fact, I need you to come to my office now, can you do that?"

Frustrated, Judith banged down the handset. She definitely did not want to act as School Secretary for the day but she felt she owed Pat. So, she had no choice, she had to go to the principal right away.

"But I will stand up for my rights," Judith asserted. "I'm determined to fight for my holiday time!" She smoothed her hair back from her face, it was brown like her eyes, and tended to frizz if not kept under control. Judith usually didn't much bother about her appearance – so long as she was clean and tidy – but right now it was important not to look frazzled. She wanted to present a calm but determined demeanor. Hurrying to the suite at the end of the corridor she planned her arguments along the way.

The moment she arrived in the principal's office Judith realized her time off was going to be cancelled for sure. It was obvious that Pat was sick, her face damp with the sheen of fever and her eyes dull. Judith was torn between sympathy for Pat's plight and her own self-pity. She resigned herself to hear disappointing news.

Lila Morelli, the school's nurse, entered the room a few moments later saying:

"You've caught the flu, Principal Johnson. And on top of the tragic news about poor Holly Lezinski, too. Your resistance will be really low."

Judith had met the new hire earlier in the month. As school bursar it was her job to put together Ms. Morelli's employment orientation package of passcodes, tax forms, and benefits. Afterwards Lila lingered but Judith had no interest in small talk or coworker gossip and hurried her on her way. Seeing Lila in professional mode was interesting.

"Professional except for the hair, that is." Judith amended, eyeing the turquoise streaks in Lila's blonde pageboy.

Nurse Morelli wore a white medical jacket over regular clothes, not scrubs or a uniform. She pulled a digital thermometer out of her pocket and checked the older woman's temperature at wrist and then at forehead.

"Normal temp, no fever," she announced.

Judith perked up at the happy news, saying:

"Great, not flu then."

But Lila shook her head answering:

"No, that doesn't mean no flu it simply means the virus can thrive instead of breaking with a high temperature. When the fever hits, and it almost definitely will, you'll be better off in bed. Principal Johnson is there anyone at home, or who could come to your home, to keep an eye on you?"

"Oh yes, yes really, I'm okay. There's no need to fuss. My husband took early retirement to pursue his hobbies from home. He'll look after me."

She struggled to get up and both women hurried to give assistance. Frail and shaky – this was not the Patricia Johnson Judith was used to seeing!

"Judith, you'll follow the usual procedure and step in for me?" Pat pleaded.

Judith struggled to keep her thoughts from showing on her face. She hadn't want to take over the secretary's job and now it looked like she was getting the added burden of the principal's duties. She wanted to take her vacation break! However...

"Of course, Pat. Don't worry about a thing, just concentrate on getting better. We'll be fine," she soothed.

Turning to Lila Morelli she added:

"Well, Nurse Morelli, I'm afraid you'll have to help me while both Samira and Principal Johnson are absent." Judith resented sounding petulant. She spotted Lila Morelli's poorly disguised smirk and was surprised to find herself smiling back.

"Well, Bursar Taylor, since we've been thrown together, I suggest you call me Lila. Sound good, Judith?"

Chapter Three

Judith was busy studying the more extensive calendar, filled with appointments and class schedules, in the principal's office when Lila returned from helping Patricia Johnson into her car.

The principal had insisted on driving it home since she and her husband only had the one vehicle. Lila tried to organize one teacher to drive and another to follow in their own car, but Pat resisted getting anyone else involved. Judith had listened to the exchange without comment, she knew Pat was stubborn so there was no point arguing.

"Principal Johnson has given us a dozen things to do, most of which won't get done, but she had one very good suggestion," said Lila. "We can direct all the incoming phone calls to the staff room phone. That way everything will get picked up by the answering machine. She explained how it's done and it's a simple redirect."

"Yes of course, I forgot about that. It's something Samira does but not often."

Judith told Lila how the protocol had been established years before and was carried out whenever the admin office was unable to answer calls.

"Since the staff can't be expected to take down messages – some of which are quite lengthy! – while enjoying their well-deserved break every caller is asked to leave their information.

If someone in the break-room is expecting a call they are able to pick up the handset and have their conversation. The only drawback to the system is that anyone and everyone can hear the messages. People have warned friends and family about this and to be discreet, but people forget, and some calls are definitely amusing!"

"It sounds like a good idea and something we can definitely use for the rest of the semester."

"I think we're going to have to cancel classes and start the holidays a day or so early," said Judith. "So many staff and students are off sick. And now, with the news of Holly's death, I don't think the students will be able to concentrate. I'm sure even the teachers will be gossiping about it. "

"Well, from what I remember of my school days not a lot got done in the time before Christmas anyhow."

"No, there are no exams or anything. The younger children make Christmas cards and chains out of construction paper. The middle group read Christmas stories, and the older girls are busy preparing for the play. Oh no, Holly had a starring role in the play!"

"This is my first Christmas here, so I don't know how important the play is--"

"It matters," interrupted Judith, "but with this flu bug going 'round we'll have to cancel the performance. Some of the cast are sick already and to sit in a closed room with a bunch of people who are sniffling, sneezing, and coughing... ugh! It will have to be rescheduled for some time in the New Year. Can't be helped."

"What play are they doing?"

"Their own. Noel Larkin – have you met him yet? – he's the Drama teacher and he gets them to write a script, play the parts, make costumes and scenery, everything in fact. It always has some sort of a Christmas theme. The parents love it."

"I do know Noel, he's invited me to his Christmas party, along with the rest of the staff, that is."

"Yes, it's a combination birthday and Christmas event. He was actually born on the 25th hence the name choice."

"I like the name Noel, it's unusual. And he seems like a nice guy, in fact considering how good-looking he is he's surprisingly nice."

"Hmm, never thought of him that way but you're right he is a nice man."

"And handsome too, remember," said Lila with a smile and a question in her voice. Judith wasn't paying attention; she was too busy studying the big calendar. She self-described as 'detail-oriented' and was reading every entry. She replied offhandedly:

"If you like the 'male model' type, then sure."

"Ha, that does fit him. So do you prefer the rugged he-man type?" Lila teased.

"I don't have a type," Judith retorted.

"'Okay Lila don't go there', I get it."

Judith rolled her eyes, saying: "I'm just not interested."

"So, is the party a fun thing? or does it feel like a work outing?"

"I don't know, I've never gone."

"Oh, sorry, I thought everyone was invited."

"Well of course I'm always invited, yes, but I don't mix with my coworkers as a rule."

Lila answered using a pretend-whiny tone: "Does that mean you won't go with me to show me the ropes, as it were?"

"I wouldn't know the 'ropes' if I tripped over them." Judith caught herself smiling, enjoying this unaccustomed banter. She found that she couldn't help but like Lila.

"Besides, when it comes to socializing with coworkers, I think you'll find the teachers consider themselves a cut above the rest of the staff. They seem friendly but they aren't exactly welcoming," Judith said with a shrug, "Maybe things will be different for you."

Lila sidestepped that comment by asking: "So how do we go about cancelling the rest of the school year?"

"We'll get everyone into the auditorium and make an announcement--"

"Yes, Principal Johnson wanted us to tell the girls about Holly and have a minute's silence. We can combine that with notice about the school closure."

"Well, that's the other thing. Many of the parents are at work during the day so we have to give them some notice before sending the girls home. The best thing to do is have the school open for the next couple of days, but attendance can be optional. For the students, that is, the teachers will still have to come in. Then, depending on how many students show up, we can decide to stay open or close.

For sure we'll close on the 24th. Usually, we're open for a half-day of snacks and socializing, card and gift exchanges, and then the school play takes place in the afternoon. This year we'll just have to tell everyone to stay home. I don't think even a small party would be appropriate."

"Oh, do you think Noel will cancel his party?"

"No, and nobody would expect him to do so. But it's different for the school. Holly was one of us and the parents expect us to observe the proprieties."

"You're in charge, Judith, so get on the PA system and call everyone to the assembly. I'll go organize the chairs into rows."

With Lila gone Judith took a moment to gear herself up. The announcement was no problem, she could easily speak into the microphone, but standing up to give a speech in front of the entire school? well... she'd accept her responsibilities but that sort of thing wasn't in her job description.

Chapter Four

As Edgemont village grew into a small town the local school needed a newer and bigger building. Thus, the old school became Edgemont School for Girls, which offered classes up to and including Grade Nine.

Graduating girls, usually finishing by age fifteen sometimes sixteen, went on to public or private high-schools. It served the community and surrounding area with at least one quarter of the students subsidized through donations and fundraising.

The elderly building was hard to heat in the winter, but for that season Principal Johnson had added leotards instead of knee socks to the dress code.

It was a day-school only, no one boarded.

Everyone admired the old school's style, character, and architectural details. It was built from sandstone in the Tudor/Gothic-Revival style sometime in the early 1930s.

There were no windows in the classrooms which were built in a circle inside the building. To get from one class to another the students crossed through a centre hub. One wall of windows was sectioned off to include the administrative offices, library, cafeteria, and auditorium. Indoor Phys Ed. classes were taken in the basement where a year-round chill kept the girls moving quickly in their exercises and games.

Judith shared her office with the librarian, a young woman called Cindy Callahan. Not for too much longer though since she'd received an engagement ring as an early Christmas present and would be known as Mrs. Thiessen in the future.

Cindy only worked in the library part-time since she also taught some English classes. While showing off her ring in the staff room, she'd shared her disappointment at Judith's lack of interest in the upcoming nuptials.

Cindy wanted to discuss ideal wedding dates and venues and look at Bride magazines for dresses and colour schemes, and rehash exactly Eric had said when he'd proposed... but Judith had been quite rude about 'all this chatter'. The other teachers agreed that Judith Taylor was an unfeeling woman with a cold heart.

Full of indignation Cindy had repeated all of this to Judith only this morning, after brooding about it overnight, and Judith had looked at her saying:

"How do you expect me to respond to that?"

So, the two of them spent the rest of the morning in a silence that was frosty on one side and indifferent on the other until Principal Johnson phoned.

When Judith called everyone to assemble a few raised eyebrows were exchanged along with mutters of 'what's she up to?'

Lila told the older girls to help set out chairs and instructed the rest to be seated. Everyone was asking questions, some in whispers and some out loud. After a few minutes Judith came in and walked purposely to the front of the room. She looked at the notes she'd hastily written and addressed the audience which all of a sudden seemed huge and the room overfull.

"I have several announcements to make," she said.

"Where's Principal Johnson?" called out Marta Smith, a senior teacher close to retirement age. Judith suspected Marta was going to be trouble, it was in the older woman's nature.

"The first point I have to make is about Principal Johnson so please hold your questions until I've finished," was Judith's curt reply.

"Principal Johnson has appointed me in charge temporarily. She's sick with this flu bug that's going around and had to go home. As did her secretary, Ms. Kanji. Nurse Morelli is assisting me. That's the first item." She had to raise her voice over a mumbling of complaint from the teachers.

"Secondly, and this is very sad news, the police have been in touch to tell us they've found Holly Lezinsky dead."

Pandemonium as the audience gasped, cried, and shouted out in shock.

"It's an 'unlawful killing' and that's all they've told us."

Everyone knew who everyone was at Edgemont School. They would all have known Holly.

The teachers often complained that Holly was always talking back but acknowledged that the girl added wit and humour to her cheekiness which made everyone smile. The youngest students idolized her. Questions were shouted out.

"I know everyone is upset. I'm upset by this news. It's terrible, but I'm sorry I don't know anything else. The police want to talk to Holly's family – her mother – before sharing details with us. When we hear more, I will pass on that information.

And that brings me to the final announcement: the school will stay open for the next couple of days, but classes are cancelled. Teachers will be in their rooms so any students who have to come in because of working parents will be looked after. We'll decide what to do on a day-by-day basis.

We will definitely close at end-of-day on December 23rd and remain closed until our return on January 2nd. Students, you must inform your parents about the school situation."

Somebody wailed, "What about the play?" and others repeated the question.

"It will have to be performed in January–"

"But it's a Christmas play!"

"Perhaps it can be adapted for Valentine's? Mr. Larkin will work that out with you. Besides, with so many teachers, students, and parents already sick we wouldn't have had a big turnout anyhow."

"To say nothing about cancelling it in honour of poor Holly!" exclaimed Marta standing up and turning to her fellow teachers for support. But students yelled her down with shouts of 'the show must go on' and claiming, 'Holly wouldn't want it cancelled, she has an understudy to take over her role'. Marta remained on her feet only to be shamed back to her chair when Judith announced:

"We will now have a minute's silence to reflect and pray for Holly. Again, once we're back in the new year the school will have a proper memorial service for her."

This was only a moment's respite before she was bombarded by the teachers asking endless questions despite knowing that she didn't have any further news.

Many of the girls were still sniffing away tears but one child was loudly sobbing. It was Bethany Penner. Of course, she was Holly's best friend.

They were two very different types of girl who proved the 'opposites attract' statement. Beth was quiet where Holly was loud, shy and content to follow Holly's lead. Now Lila was leading the girl out of the room with an arm about her heaving shoulders.

Marta informed Judith that she'd be speaking to Principal Johnson 'right away'. Judith kept her 'good luck with that' comment to herself, knowing that Pat's husband was more than capable of fending off unwelcome intrusions.

Chapter Five

"Let's go to the staff-room and see what phone messages have come in so far."

"I'll grab coffees and meet you there – how do you take yours?"

"Milky, no sugar," said Judith then added, "Thanks," as an afterthought.

Armed with paper and pens the two women listened to the dozen or so phone-calls. News about Holly hadn't gotten out yet, so the majority of calls were from parents calling in to excuse their children from class due to sickness. The flu bug striking again and again.

Once the messages were all listened to and return calls made where necessary, they decided to compose an email to the parents.

"I want to text it as well as send an email. I don't think we need to utilize the phone tree; it's only supposed to be for emergency use. Text and email should cover everyone," said Judith.

"Yeah, texting is a good idea because many parents skip over emails from the school. We send out far too many. This school follows the directives from both the Public and Catholic school boards, so it seems like we're nagging the parents about such-and-such a social issue every other day. I know because the boards keep coming to me for input on the medical issues."

"The next biggie is money. Parents are called upon to shell out for so much. Personal school supplies like pens, erasers, pencil cases – sure – but when we're asking payment to rent textbooks? and the insurance fee for Phys Ed. has more than doubled in the last couple of years.

And then there's the fundraising: 'We want to plant trees', 'we want to have a year-end dance', 'we want to buy iPads', 'we want to sponsor a child in a Third World Country', 'we want a school trip to the Petting Zoo' ... it's no wonder the parents ignore our messages! So, we need a subject line that will grab them."

"How about 'School Closure'?" suggested Lila.

"No, they'll think it's another email about our schedule for the holidays. What about, in all caps: 'CLASSES CANCELLED.' That should get their attention, eh? and then we'll let them know the police have discovered Holly Lezinsky's body and are calling it a 'suspicious death'. We'll add that we don't know anything else—"

"No, that won't work," interrupted Lila, "because they won't read that far, they'll already be dialling their cellphones. How about if we start off by saying something like 'The school remains open until end of day December 23rd but there will be no classes and students do not have to attend.' Then we can word it like 'When the police give us more information, we will pass it on immediately. They have discovered student Holly Lezinsky's body and are calling it a 'suspicious death'. Please – in uppercase again – DO NOT PHONE THE SCHOOL. There is no one available to take your calls, we don't have answers yet anyway."

"That's good. But we'll leave out the bit saying we don't have answers because that makes it sound like we're to blame. They'll all call and leave messages asking: 'why don't you have answers?'"

Lila laughed saying, "You're right, that's exactly what they would do! Hey, should we mention the school play? You said it was important."

"God yes, the stupid play."

Lila laughed and said: "How about, 'There is no one available to take your calls and the mailbox fills up too quickly. We will give you the new date for the school play in January.'"

"Makes sense to me but they'll all assume the play will be held in January. It might, but we aren't sure. So, change that to 'we're rescheduling the school play, date TBA' and we'll just have to hope for the best."

"OK, here's the revised script: subject line: CLASSES CANCELLED. Message body:

ITEM #1 The school remains open until end of day December 23rd but there will be no classes and students do not have to attend.

ITEM #2 When the police give us more information we will pass it on immediately. They have discovered student Holly Lezinsky's body and are calling it a 'suspicious death'. Please DO NOT PHONE THE SCHOOL. There is no one available to take your calls and the mailbox fills up too quickly.

ITEM #3 We're rescheduling the school play, date TBA.'"

"That will do. Now, I'll handle the emails if you'll look after the texting. I've noticed that you're quick at it. I'm a typist trained to use all my fingers, not just my thumbs, even if the phone does provide a QWERTY keyboard."

"Sure, that works for me." Lila was agreeable as ever.

They smiled at each other, and Judith experienced an uncommon feeling of camaraderie, glad that Lila was working with her.

The women settled down to their respective tasks, pausing now and then to take a sip of coffee or to listen to yet another parent – some sounding quite frazzled – call in to say the household was struck down by the flu.

Chapter Six

"Hell of a day and that assembly was a truly horrible experience – very emotional," announced Lila, "So this medical practitioner is prescribing strong drink as a remedy to today – are you up for it?"

She was so surprised by the invitation Judith didn't even think before blurting out:

"I don't drink."

"Ever?" asked Lila with a grin.

"No, I never do."

"Not even at New Year's? or champagne at a wedding? or a frosty cold one on a hot summer's day?" Lila was smiling and not taking Judith's pronouncement seriously.

"No, I never drink alcohol or wine or spirits, cocktails, or beer – does that answer your question?" She regretted letting her annoyance show but Lila persisted.

"Why not?"

"That's none of your business." snapped Judith, reliving memories of coming home from school to find her mother passed out drunk. Mrs. Taylor was always found on the floor by the drinks cabinet where the sherry was stored. She'd gulp it straight from the bottle until she dropped to the floor in a stupor.

Judith could never bring schoolmates home and couldn't go out because someone had to take care of the drunken woman. The spectacle of her mother struggling and collapsing when Judith tried to lift her, slurring maudlin apologies, all accompanied by the stench of alcohol and vomit, combined to make Judith a committed teetotaller.

She wasn't worried that she'd become an alcoholic, she just couldn't bear the thought of becoming her mother.

"Remind me never to invite you to my parent's place, they would be totally offended if you refused a glass of their homemade wine."

"Why would you want to invite me to your parent's home?" asked Judith with a puzzled frown.

"They always like meeting my friends but I can't invite you anyhow because they live in Toronto."

"Well... that was a ridiculous... oh you!" Judith shook her head in exasperation but catching Lila's grin couldn't help but smile back.

"Okay so I know it's none of my business, but that doesn't mean I don't want to know why you don't drink."

"Hmm, but it also means I don't have to tell you."

Lila shrugged off Judith's refusal saying,

"Another time, maybe."

Judith marvelled at the other woman's persistence. Lila's strong personality and frank curiosity were like weapons. Judith would have to be careful with what she said around Lila, at least if she wanted to try to keep her – as she did with everyone else – at arms-length. She put on her coat saying,

"I'll see you tomorrow morning."

Chapter Seven

Lila managed to get out successfully, but Judith was waylaid at the front door by a rather large and very determined woman. Judith had no difficulty recognizing Andrea Sealy, mother of a nine-year-old student called Margaret.

"I got in the car the absolute moment I got your text because I knew I couldn't sleep a wink if I didn't come and see you."

"Why?" Judith stayed in the doorway, not inviting the parent to come inside, because she wanted to end this conversation and go home.

"Whatever do you mean, why?"

"If you read the whole text, you'd know that it has already told you everything. Every. Single. Thing. That's all we at the school know at this time. You've wasted a trip because there's nothing more to say."

"Oh, Ms. Taylor it's so obvious that you're not a parent."

Judith couldn't resist saying: "Apparently what?"

"What?! Oh, this is nonsense. You must have more information like was the child assaulted... you know, sexually? or beaten up? how exactly did she die? and where?"

"Mrs. Sealy this isn't a whodunit on the TV. I do not have any of that information because the police haven't shared it with me. They want to speak to Holly's mother first and quite right, too. Our school is grieving and I don't want to speculate.

The police haven't even come to the school although they did say they hope to come by at some point tomorrow. I will be here to meet with them. If they give me more information, and I very much hope that

21

they do, I will send out another round of texts and emails to all of the parents right away.

I do understand your concern, but I hope you will understand that I've had a very long and difficult day and now I want to lock up and go home."

Andrea Sealy looked like she wanted to rehash everything that had been said and then say it all over again but was thwarted by the determined look on Judith's face. She felt it would be unwise to push the other woman too far, after all she didn't want to be 'accidentally left out' of the communication loop.

Forced to live with her dissatisfaction she decided she'd leave now but would definitely have a word with Principal Johnson later on.

"Oh, very well," she said ungraciously, "I suppose I don't have any choice. Of course, I won't sleep a wink, not a wink!" When she saw Judith eyeing her fur coat she hastened to add:

"This isn't real, you know. It's a very good quality faux fur."

Judith bit her lip to hold back her comments. She didn't want to offend Andrea Sealy and she certainly didn't want to prolong the conversation. Though she wondered to herself: "Then what's the point?"

Andrea stood back to watch Judith lock the door and they each speed-walked through the chilly evening to their respective cars. Andrea Sealy stayed in hers until Judith pulled out of the parking lot and then she followed.

"Huh! no doubt she thinks I'm going to sneak back inside to gloat over some juicy tidbits that I refuse to share with her," Judith just shook her head. "What a battle-ax, I'll bet dollars to doughnuts nobody has ever gotten away with calling that one 'Andy'".

Chapter Eight

"Lila was right, that was quite a day!" thought Judith. She was tired, emotional, and anxious to get home as quickly as possible. She thought about Lila's offer of going for a drink and wondered why the other woman had made the suggestion. "Does she know something about me? I've always wondered if people do know about my background. I mean, it's not a secret but it's also not something I advertise."

Judith had an uncomfortable moment imagining Marta and the other teachers laughing behind her back in the staff room. She tried, but failed, to picture Lila being a party to such behaviour and conceded that the invitation was probably just a friendly gesture.

Andrea Sealy had swung her SUV around into the other lane to pass Judith once they were on the road. She would have missed seeing Beth Penner at the lot's entrance hanging around, weighed down by her bulky backpack and looking forlorn. Judith spotted her and when their eyes met Beth gave a half-wave and a hopeful smile.

Judith felt imposed upon. She could stop and offer the girl a lift, but she didn't want to. She felt that the last thing she could deal with right now was non-stop questions from a weepy adolescent.

Work was over – this awful day was finally over – and she yearned to go home and forget about everything and everyone school-related until tomorrow morning. Tomorrow, which was actually supposed to be the start of her holiday now postponed.

Choosing to misunderstand she gave Beth a cheery wave back then turned her head away as she drove off, determined not to look in her rear-view mirror in case the teen tried to flag her down.

A light drizzle began but only enough to need the interval setting of the windshield wipers. Driving along Judith found herself wondering why Beth's backpack was so full since there were no more homework assignments for this semester. "I hope she's got one of those telescoping umbrellas packed inside," thought Judith.

She had no idea where the girl lived, or how far she'd have to walk. She really had very little to do with the students themselves. The rain was turning to sleet as temperatures dropped even further and Judith needed to concentrate on her driving.

Chapter Nine

As soon as she got to the school in the morning Judith moved her laptop and assorted files to the principal's office. She'd just settled in with the coffee she'd picked up in the lunch-room – the school's resources didn't run to a full-service cafeteria – when Marta confronted her with the snide remark:

"Hasn't taken you long to get your bum in the big chair."

Judith tilted her head at the 'bum' comment but made no reply. In the silence Marta blurted out the reason for her visit:

"I want to meet with the police when they come."

"That will be up to the police, of course. I can't – and won't – tell them what to do, and neither would Principal Johnson."

"Hmph, well I don't know about that but anyhow, when are they coming?"

"No one has told me."

Marta thought about this a moment then turned to go saying:

"You better let me know when they get here."

Again, Judith said nothing, and the older woman flounced out of the room almost colliding with the young woman who had arrived and was lifting her hand to knock.

"Annalise! what are you doing here?" Marta demanded to know.

"I wanted to see Judith if she's not too busy..." Annalise's voice, always low-pitched, trailed off in uncertainty.

"Please come in, Annalise. Sit down and tell me what it is you wanted to see me about." Seeing that Marta was still hovering in the doorway she added: "Marta is leaving now."

Judith had a chance to study Annalise while the girl – it was hard to think of her as a woman – removed her outdoor things and got settled in a chair. She was very fair, very feminine, slender, and youthful. She could pass for sixteen, but Judith knew she was eight years older than that.

Annalise Sutherland came from enormous wealth and Judith was certain that a chauffeur driving a luxury car was waiting at the front door.

Annalise and Noel Larkin were engaged to be married in the coming year, and it was on his behalf that she said she was visiting:

"Noel is so upset by what happened to that girl, Holly. He knew her, you see, because of the school play. She had the leading role and so they were thrown together a lot and he told me he quite liked her." Annalise sounded surprised. "Naturally he's devastated by her death. Or should I say her murder?" she asked in a questioning tone.

Judith had no idea what kind of response was expected of her, so she made a non-committal 'mmh-mmh' sound and that was all the encouragement Annalise needed:

"He's such a sensitive man. I'm the first to admit that Noel will turn his back on any unpleasantness and that's okay because I'm not confrontational either. We're both gentle souls – that's what he says – and our hearts are easily bruised."

Judith was growing more and more confused by the conversation: she couldn't see any point to it.

"Do you think there's something I can do to help you? or Noel? or both of you together?" she offered.

"Yes, actually. We would so, so appreciate it if you could see that both of our names are kept out of the papers. Daddy would be awfully upset. Also, Noel tells me that this Holly is a bit of a fantasist. Well, that's how he puts it but to me it sounds like she's a little liar.

I met her you know. A few times I've dropped in on rehearsals – to give Noel my support, you know – and Holly seemed to take the playacting to heart. She was very dramatic and, frankly, overly familiar with him, the little minx. She had a huge crush on Noel. I wouldn't like anyone, like the police, to get the wrong impression."

"In other words, if anyone connects Noel to Holly, I'm to put a stop to any talk of that kind."

"Exactly. You understand me completely," the young woman gave a sweet smile.

"Yes, Annalise, I do understand you." Annalise didn't notice Judith's dry tone as she continued:

"This is such a weight off my mind, and it will be for Noel too. He'll be so relieved, and so will his mother. You see, Holly had even started phoning him at home!

His mother told me she had the nerve to ask to leave a message for him to call her back. Now, you and I wouldn't think that's a big deal, but Audrey Larkin was beside herself! She complained that it was awful behaviour and so rude to expect her to write out a message. You do know Holly Lezinsky is – was – one of the girls they sponsor, right? Anyhow, because she considered it such an imposition Noel had to speak to Holly and tell her not to phone again. After that Mrs. Larkin said she started to get lots of hang-ups whenever she answered a call.

Of course she put two and two together. It was all very unpleasant. Teenagers do have such a difficult time with all their emotions running rampant and wanting, so desperately, to be grown up."

"If they only knew, eh?" replied Judith.

"Too true! Anyhow, I won't keep you a minute more. Only this morning I was telling Noel that it's wonderful the way you've stepped into Principal Johnson's shoes at this difficult time."

Annalise put her fur coat back on ("This is definitely a real one," thought Judith) although the waiting car would be toasty warm. They said their goodbyes and then Annalise was gone leaving nothing but her expensive perfume lingering in the air.

Noel and Holly had been staying after school quite a bit recently while they finished rehearsing their play. Under those circumstances Judith had never given their behaviour a second thought. Now that Annalise had drawn attention to the relationship, and commented about the police, it framed everything in a different context and Judith found herself wondering.

Chapter Ten

Marta had been hanging around outside the closed door to the principal's office waiting for Annalise to leave. When Judith realized this, she couldn't help but wonder how much poking and prying Marta had indulged in at the secretary's desk.

It was satisfying for her to know that the snoopy teacher could find nothing since Samira kept her drawers locked, with no key lying about.

As soon as the young woman left Marta immediately came into the office, not even bothering to knock.

"Well, what did she want?" she asked, not bothering to mask her impatience.

"Marta, what do you want?" said Judith, feeling exasperated.

"I want to know when the police are coming because I need to speak to them, they should know that--" sensing someone behind her she turned around to see a man and woman standing outside the door.

"Are you the police?" Marta demanded to know.

"Are you in charge here Mrs.--" replied the man before Marta interrupted with a correction:

"Ms. Smith, Ms. Marta Smith, and I'm the Senior Teacher here at Edgemont School for Girls."

"Well, I hope you can spare some time for us later but right now we need to meet with the school's Acting Head a.." he glanced at a notebook in his hand before continuing, "Ms. Taylor."

"I'm Judith Taylor," announced Judith stepping forward to greet the officers who manoeuvred Marta out of the doorway and into the hall while moving forward to shake hands.

"I'm George Grant, Senior Investigating Officer, and this is my partner, Suzanne Mirteau."

"He's tall but aren't all police?" thought Judith as they exchanged greetings and business cards. She continued commenting to herself, "She's tall as well. They make me feel quite short but I'm not, I'm a bit taller than average height."

The three of them then moved into the sitting area of the room. Judith's offer of coffee was declined and when Suzanne brought out her notebook Judith produced her own asking if she could get a quick re-cap of the facts since many people were asking questions.

George Grant looked to be about forty years old. Judging by the laugh lines around his mouth and eyes he had a sense of humour, and his frank gaze spoke to an open, friendly demeanor. He answered saying:

"I expected as much and have thought about how much we can share with you."

"Since you're only a member of the public," interjected Suzanne. She was about a dozen years younger than him and a good-looking woman. George gave her a brief look then resumed saying,

"Here are the basic facts: The body of Holly Lezinsky was found by a woman named Kellogg walking her dogs in the wooded area that borders the school property but at the far side of it. The trails there are popular with joggers and dog-walkers. She told us she'd taken her animals to the same area early in the morning and there definitely was no sign of young Holly then. Based on this, the second walk of the day, we concluded the actual discovery must have happened between 11:00

– roughly – when Mrs. Kellogg arrived until 11:10 when she phoned the Emergency Services."

"Holly was killed in School Woods?"

"I didn't realize the area had a name."

"Well, it's what we've always called them. The girls are often in the woods: taking pathways home, playing at 'forest bathing', Natural Science classes... It's horrible to think of Holly dying there. And so close by to us, too. I hope she wasn't lying there dying and we never knew!"

"We don't think that's the murder scene, actually," said George. Suzanne made an annoyed sound at his revelation at the same time Judith gasped:

"Murdered? For sure? We thought it might have been some sort of accident or... well, suicide."

"Was Holly–– you did know her, right?"

"Yes, yes I did."

"Would you consider her at risk of committing suicide?"

"Not at all but I guess it just seems well... a teenage thing and somehow better than being murdered... oh, that doesn't make sense."

Suzanne's snort indicated she agreed but George's voice was soothing:

"It does make sense. Murder belongs in the pages of a book or on the big screen, right? We do understand what a shock it is for the average person."

"Members of the public," put in Suzanne again before turning to George and saying: "I'm not sure you should be telling her all this, Grant."

Judith found Suzanne Mirteau abrasive but even so thought it odd that she'd call her superior by his surname.

Judith had noticed that with him being white-blond and her having wavy black hair the two of them made a striking, good-looking pair, but it was obvious they weren't a couple. Despite the fact that Suzanne's gaze kept turning towards him, George Grant was all business.

Although Judith did notice him looking at the bare fingers of her left hand. When she looked up she saw that Suzanne noticed this as well and her face wore a sour expression.

"Ms. Taylor I'm giving you the same facts I discussed yesterday with Holly's family. Actually, it's just her mother, Dana, and her boyfriend." He paused and Suzanne supplied the name:

"Billy MacNeill."

"Yes, thank you. I know that once the family has been told word starts to get around and sometimes things are exaggerated or misunderstood because, understandably, it's such a very difficult time for a parent. It's hard for them to absorb everything."

"How did she die?"

"We can't be certain until after the autopsy, but she had received a severe blow to the back of her head that is likely to be the cause of death."

"Couldn't she have fallen and hit her head against something?"

"We're not here to speculate with you, Ms. Taylor," snapped Suzanne. Judith was puzzled at the woman's antagonism and George ignored the comment replying:

"We won't know anything definite until we hear back from the Medical Examiner. So yes, it could have been an accidental fall or even a push with fatal consequences but moving the body was a deliberate act to conceal evidence and that's a crime.

In our opinion, murder is most likely the answer."

"Yes, I see. Thank you for being forthright."

George stood to go, and Judith was taken aback by the warm smile he gave her. Glancing over at Suzanne she saw from the angry expression on the woman's face that she hadn't missed that exchange either. Judith didn't understand all the tension happening underneath the surface remarks and actions.

"That's all I can tell you right now. When people ask questions you can let them know that the police are treating the death as suspicious but that the actual cause hasn't been determined yet. We'll have more information by tomorrow and I can give you an update then."

"I appreciate you explaining this to me and thank you Inspector Grant. I will be here at the school all day tomorrow, but we might not have any students. If there are no classes the front door will be locked and you'll have to phone first so I can let you in."

"Okay, I've got the school's phone number."

"No, um I better give you my cellphone number. The school's phone is switched over to the staff-room and I won't hear it. For example, I'm sure there have been plenty of calls already today and we didn't hear any ringing from here."

"I'm certain you've got a busy day ahead of you, so we'll leave you to it. I'll take note of your number and if you can point us in the right direction, we'll go to the staff-room now to see Ms. Smith. I hope she won't be too annoyed at the delay."

Judith returned his smile saying: "As long as you call it the Teachers' Lounge instead of the staff-room, you'll be fine."

He copied down her phone number then followed Suzanne. He stopped in the doorway and turned back to Judith saying:

"Just 'Grant' is fine, that's what everyone calls me, you don't need to give me a title, and I don't use my first name."

Judith wondered why he was telling her this and, once again, was puzzled by Suzanne's glare.

Chapter Eleven

Lila came into the office the moment the police left it. She was full of questions about what they were like, what had been said, and what would happen next. Judith started from when they'd met Marta and recounted the whole interview.

"The body was moved? Poor Holly. So that happened by mid-morning. When did she die, by the way? She was gone a week or more."

"They didn't say how long she'd been dead for, and I didn't ask. Actually, I didn't ask any questions, that female officer was so mean and angry and resented every scrap of information Grant gave."

"Grant?"

"Mmm, Senior Investigating Officer George Grant who said he only goes by 'Grant' so that's what I'm to call him."

"Oh, I thought you were on first-name terms already," said Lila was a grin.

"Certainly not! He calls me Ms. Taylor." Judith ignored Lila's chuckle and continued:

"I figured he'd tell me more if I didn't ask questions so although it's not much we now know that Holly was likely murdered, not sure when, and her body was moved to School Woods this morning where it was found by a Mrs. Kellogg and her dogs."

"She was in our woods? Had she been raped? Was she naked? Strangled or stabbed or..."

"Nothing was said about any of that. What a vivid imagination you have! They did say that there was evidence of a 'severe blow' to her head and that's all that was mentioned."

"Aha, the infamous blunt instrument."

"Lila it's no laughing matter," cried Judith. Right away Lila drew closer and reached for Judith's hand saying,

"I'm so sorry. Most of us in the medical profession use humour to get us over the bad bits. But I'm sure it sounds ghoulish and unfeeling to non-medicos, and I truly do apologise."

Judith pulled her hand out of reach and told Lila she understood.

"So, an autopsy. Well, I guess the truth will come out then so I will tell you now what Holly told me in confidence the last time I saw her, which was the day she disappeared: she was pregnant."

"But she would just be turning fourteen this week!" exclaimed Judith.

"It might not be true, but she said she was and I have no reason to doubt her. She didn't come right out and announce it to me but when I noticed she was very pale and drawn looking – I wondered about anaemia – she said she figured it was her condition, being pregnant and all, and that she felt fine."

"That is shocking. It means she was thirteen when..."

"I barely knew her and I might have misjudged based on appearances but I wasn't floored by the revelation. I mean, thirteen is shockingly young but Holly doesn't, I mean didn't, seem like a thirteen-year-old girl."

"I know what you mean. Any mother, of girls or boys, would be worried about Holly being a bad influence but they'd still find themselves liking the girl despite it all. I wonder who the father is?"

"Isn't that the $20,000 question!"

Chapter Twelve

The trailer park was a surprise. Judith couldn't say what she'd expected but it wasn't this. There was nothing transient-looking about the place. No rusting-out vehicles or abandoned broken toys. The trailers were trim, and the yards were tidy. Most had hanging baskets for flowers, and one even had a quaint white picket fence. Strings of Christmas lights and inflatable lawn ornaments indicated it would be festive at night.

The trailer where Holly lived with her mother wasn't as nicely kept as those around it. The windows could do with a cleaning and the metal steps leading to the door were flaking with rust. However, inside the air was fresh and warm with the appetizing smell of home baking.

When Dana Lezinsky saw Judith sniff she turned and pointed to a wire-rack piled high with iced cookies.

"I always make them for her birthday, and I went ahead and made them as usual before I remembered. These pineapple cookies were her favourite." She opened the cupboard above the counter and pulled out a plate. "I've made coffee," she announced, "Go ahead and take a seat and I'll bring everything over."

There was a small table with attached bench seating, similar to a booth in a cafe. Everything in the trailer had a compact, space-saving design. Judith could imagine herself living quite cozily and comfortably in such a home.

Judith studied Dana while the woman filled up the plate with cookies and moved back and forth from fridge to counter to table with cups, a carafe of coffee, milk jug, sugar bowl, and spoons. Laying out the dishes with almost ritual precision.

She looked to be in her late 20s or early 30s which meant she had been a teenager when she had Holly. Judith knew from the records she kept for the school that Dana was a hairdresser and her income qualified Holly for the subsidy programme.

There was no money coming from the girl's father – he wasn't even given a name – and no mention of a boyfriend in the file.

Dana looked devastated by Holly's death and Judith realized the trauma actually had begun a week earlier when the girl went missing.

Dana looked like she hadn't slept during that whole week. Her hair was dirty enough to stand on end where she'd raked her fingers through it, the trails clearly showing. Her face was gray and sagging with a drooping mouth and swollen red-rimmed eyes. She must have been given tranquilizers because she was slow-moving and had trouble focusing.

The woman oozed sadness and despair. Judith felt terribly sorry for her but didn't know how to express her feelings. She thought it best to sit in shared silence until Dana was ready to speak. She ate a cookie murmuring 'mmm' sounds.

"I asked to see you because you were always nice to me. You spoke straight when we met about my finances, and you didn't talk down. Not like most of the mothers at that school do. That's why I don't, um... didn't, like going to those get-togethers and the parent-teacher meetings? they were always an ordeal." Dana's voice held little inflection, but she didn't mumble, and her meaning was clear.

"I'm not a parent, do you think that makes a difference? maybe makes it seem easier to talk to me?" asked Judith.

"I don't know... maybe. The police were here again this morning. They were here twice yesterday, to break the news of find... finding Holly and then they had to come back again later because I was too upset to talk first time.

Anyhow, they were good. A man cop and a woman and she didn't say much but he was nice. But this morning they came back and after what they told me well, I felt utterly destroyed. They said my baby was going to have a baby: Holly was pregnant!"

"Oh no."

"Yes, and that means some bastard got her pregnant when she was only thirteen years old! That's illegal, that is. It's interfering with a child, child endangerment, stuff like that. I mean, I was young when I had her, but I sure wasn't that young, and her Daddy was the same age or thereabouts."

"Is he around, her Dad? can he give you some support while you're going through this?"

"Naw, I'm not even sure who fathered her. I meant that there were a few boys, several of them, and we were all at school together, so we were all the same age."

"Holly was a very popular girl–"

"Oh, I know she had boyfriends, she was a pretty girl who wasn't backward about coming forward – have you heard that expression? it might have been written for her.

So, I know the boys were hanging around, but I told her and told her to be careful and she always said she didn't waste her time on 'kids', that's how she put it, called the boys who came by 'kids' and said they had no money, no car, and she wasn't interested in them.

They'd be out sitting on those picnic tables in that bit of a park across from us here and I could see them from the window.

I'd see kids smoking – probably drinking too – making some noise but not causing trouble. The manager of this place is pretty strict in dealing with problem people but he's a good guy and knows kids have to let off a bit of steam.

So, things were always under control and it seemed like Holly treated everyone, girls and guys, the same. They were all friends hanging out."

Dana became more animated as she spoke. Judith could see in her face that she was recalling images and conversations, and these were good memories. All of a sudden her mood changed and with it her body language too. Shoulders drooped and her head sunk down towards her chest. The next words were spoken in a low voice and Judith had to strain to hear.

"That's when I wondered what if Billy had done something to her? Or not him but friends of his? he was always teasing Holly and depending on how she was feeling she flirted back, or she shut him up quick. That's all I ever saw between them, the two of them talking shit, you know? but what if I missed something? what if he saw her away from here?"

"Well, he sometimes picked her up from school in his truck," said Judith.

"I knew about that, yeah, that was OK."

"And then there was the fight they had two or three weeks ago."

"A fight?!"

"Not a fight... more like a boyfr–uh brother-sister type of quarrel," Judith was quick to amend her poor choice of words.

"What happened?"

"I don't know what it was about or anything, I could hear their voices but not the actual words, it was the yelling that got my attention and when I looked out I saw Billy grabbing Holly by the arm and flinging her in the truck."

"He took her against her will?" cried Dana.

"No, because he slammed the door but her seat-belt or something must have caught because the door sprang back open. He didn't notice, he was already marching round to his door, but she then moved whatever was blocking and pulled the door closed herself.

She would have gotten out and run back to the school if she'd thought she was in danger. So no, it was just a very heated argument between the two of them. Otherwise, I would have done something."

In truth Judith doubted she would actually have done anything. At the time, listening to the screeching and swearing she'd thought 'trailer trash' to herself and dismissed the incident.

"Well, I'm not so sure. This is why I called you to come talk to me – and that was before I even knew about this fight they had. But anyhow after the cops told me about her being pregnant and asking who she was seeing and me telling them there was nobody in particular I got to thinking. If she thought the local boys were kids was that because there was a man she was comparing them to? A man who had some spending cash and could drive her places.

I got thinking that maybe Billy MacNeill was that man and, well... this is the hard part, you see I lied to the cops when they were checking up on us, on where we were and that. So, I was hoping I could tell you and you could tell them?

I know what I did was wrong but I never in a million years suspected Billy of having anything to do with Holly disappearing and then being killed so I figured it was okay to go along with his story. I still don't think he hurt her but now that I've found out she was pregnant I don't think I can cover for him anymore and I don't want to.

If he got my baby pregnant.... I don't even want to see his face even if he wasn't the one who hurt her. I'm done with him."

Dana sat back, nodding to herself and repeating that last statement. Confessing had done her good, she sat straighter and topped up both of their coffee cups. She even ate a cookie.

"I can tell that to the police if you like, but they won't be satisfied taking my word for it. They'll still want to talk to you."

"I know, but now that I've admitted it to someone it will be easier to admit it to them. And I knew you wouldn't tell me I was a bad mother for lying. I honestly wouldn't have lied if I'd thought for one minute that he had anything to do with Holly's death. I'm sure he didn't, and really? I don't even think he's the one who got her pregnant. I don't see how they'd have managed it."

Judith accepted her statement having had a similar experience when she was a girl. Her mother, Maureen, only had the one boyfriend, and he never showed any interest in Judith. That was the only thing about him that she liked.

Her mother thought they should feel thankful and be grateful that he took care of them but not Judith. She figured he got what he wanted and nobody owed anybody anything.

She was six when her father died. He and her mother had been very happy and very much in love, and Judith had wonderful, though hazy, memories of the three of them together. When the news came about the car crash, they were both devastated. A multiple-car smash-up but only one fatality.

Her mother never recovered from the shock with only alcohol numbing the pain of her loss. Judith had nothing to help her through her grief.

Maureen kept on with her job as secretary to the man she inevitably welcomed into her bed. Judith decided it was payback for all the times he covered up for her hungover mornings. No doubt there were afternoon problems as well after a liquid lunch. He also helped out financially although the house was paid for by an insurance payout of the mortgage.

Jack was married, of course, and that suited Maureen who didn't seem to want anything more from life.

He did notice Judith and sometimes paid her compliments, but she never felt threatened. When he came by, which occurred less and less as the years progressed, often as not he and her mother would sit in front of the TV. She'd make a fuss about fixing him a drink and finding him a snack. Sometimes they'd go into Maureen's bedroom, but they didn't stay long.

Judith grew to understand that what happened then was the sex she learned about in Health class. She would listen carefully but only ever heard murmuring voices and then a sharp yelp from Jack. Immediately afterwards her mother would hurry out of the bedroom and into the bathroom. Judith was not intrigued by any of it.

When Jack retired Maureen was out of a job. She sold the house, so she and Judith had something to live on which they did as cheaply as possible. Judith was an orphan by her senior year of high school when Maureen's damaged liver finally gave out.

Judith's grades got her into a university accounting programme and her status of no family support meant a full scholarship. She mourned the mother of her six-year-old self – she had always missed her desperately

– but she had long ago stopped loving the woman Maureen had grown into.

These thoughts flitted through her mind as she finished her coffee and prepared to leave. Admitting to her lie had given Dana some sort of catharsis and after a huge yawn the woman looked like she could finally sleep. Judith wished her well and left.

Chapter Thirteen

When Judith returned to the school Marta was waiting for her, sitting in Principal Johnson's chair. She didn't get up and Judith wouldn't give her satisfaction by sitting in the visitor's chair. Before she could say a word Marta complained that the phone had been ringing non-stop.

"That's why we switched it through to the staff room, so that the machine could take messages."

"Well in my opinion it's unprofessional for a school phone to be answered that way. Also, the Teachers' Lounge is for the teachers to refresh and relax in, not be pestered by the constant ringing of the phone."

"Do you have anything to report?"

"As a matter of fact, the police came back here because they had news. They were surprised that you weren't around, in fact the 'handsome detective' looked disappointed."

"Hmm, what did they have to say?"

"I don't know, do I?" retorted the teacher in a savage tone. "That woman detective just cut me off mid-sentence saying Grant preferred 'communicating' with one person only which means you since you're the liaison between the police and this school. That's an utter joke because I should be the school's second-in-command, not you!"

"What time did they stop by?"

"I'm not your secretary, you know."

Judith wanted to shake the older woman but instead she rudely replied:

"Well then get out of the office and go do your own job. I want to talk to the police, and I'd like privacy to do so."

Marta sputtered in rage, but Lila arrived before she could spit out whatever she wanted to say.

"Lila, grand! Marta's leaving so please close the door after her I need to have a confidential talk with you about your patient."

"Certainly," Lila replied crisply, holding the doorknob and gesturing Marta out of the room. The teacher left in a temper.

"Phew, you've made an enemy there," said Lila, sitting down while Judith took the recently vacated chair behind the desk.

"Oh, never mind her, that's an old grudge. Anyhow, I wanted to talk to you about my visit with Dana Lezinsky. She had a few interesting items to report. Oh, but you know what? she'd baked cookies for Holly's birthday tomorrow before she remembered. Isn't that awful?"

"It sure is. Poor, poor woman. I can't imagine what she's going through. I've never lost anyone close to me. I mean, there were a couple of elderly aunties, but I'd never met them so the only thing their passing meant to me was getting a pendant with an opal. They lived in Australia you see, which is why we never met, and of course I didn't go to their funerals.

Anyhow, I'm babbling, I get this way. What were you going to tell me about Holly?"

"The autopsy did reveal the pregnancy, so the police know and have told Holly's mother. She was shocked by the news and she's right; you know, Holly would only have been thirteen at the time so it was a criminal act unless the baby's father is also thirteen or fourteen. Is that likely?"

"It's possible but not too likely. Does Mrs. Lezinsky have any ideas about who might be the father?"

"Well, there's a mystery there. First off, Dana had no illusions about her girl. She knew Holly was outgoing and outspoken, but she also knew that Holly wasn't interested in any of the boys who hung around her. Holly said they were 'just kids'. That's led Dana to believe Holly was involved with some man and, well, the first man who comes to mind is Dana's own boyfriend Billy MacNeill."

"Oh, eewww. She must feel awful about that."

"More like angry, even though she says she doesn't think he was the one. However, she did lie for him and that's why she called me to come over. She wants me to tell the police that she faked an alibi for him but, now that she's discovered about the pregnancy she's recanting."

"If he asked her to lie, he must have something to hide."

"But that something might not have anything to do with what happened to Holly. Unless the police pick him up first, he's going to get quite a reception when he comes home! For starters he'll find out that it's not his home anymore."

"Serves him right!"

"Agreed, but actually Dana doesn't think Billy is the father. It might seem like Holly went her own way, but Dana kept a pretty close watch on her. She knew Billy sometimes picked the girl up from school and knew what time they'd be home. I don't think he had much opportunity."

"Yeah, but she works, right? There were times when she couldn't be there herself."

"True, but Holly usually stayed late at school because of rehearsals for the play and then she and Beth Penner would walk home together. I don't think Holly had a lot of spare time between leaving school and her mother getting home from work."

"Perhaps not but somebody got that girl pregnant, and this Billy seems like a strong possibility. It only takes one time."

"What a mess this is. As if poor Dana Lezinsky doesn't have enough pain right now."

"True, and she could use some support because she's got to bury her daughter and plan a funeral and all that stuff. It's a lousy time for her boyfriend's true colours to show. I should visit her in my role as School Nurse and see if I can help her out."

"She might have taken him back by then, but it sounds like a good idea. And it's nice of you. Better you than me!"

"I can tell you're not a hugger!"

"You've got that right! Anyhow according to Marta the phone has been ringing off the hook so I wonder if we should call a parents' meeting to give an update? Something informal, basically an opportunity for us to pass on the little that we do know and then to let them have their say. What do you think?"

"Good idea, but it will have to be soon. It's already the 20th and people have plans at this time of year."

"Oh, I don't care if anyone shows up – in fact I'd like it better if they didn't! but I want to make the offer."

Lila laughed at that. "When I came to the office, I heard you telling Marta Smith that you had to call the police so I will leave you to it. Let me know what they say, okay? and then we can send out another round of messages to the parents inviting them to join us for a chat."

"Sounds good to me, and please close the door after you."

Chapter Fourteen

Judith was well-organized, as always, and located Grant's business card right away. Once she got him on the line she started to explain about meeting with Dana Lezinsky and her revelations, but Grant interrupted to say he'd come right over to get a statement from her in person. He arrived quickly but unfortunately had Suzanne Mirteau in tow.

"Good afternoon, Ms. Taylor."

"Good afternoon, um, Grant," Judith replied. Suzanne stood beside her boss smirking. "Please sit down, both of you. We're all busy so I'll get straight to the point. Holly's mother, Dana Lezinsky, told me about–"

"Sorry to interrupt but can we start at the beginning? How did you come to be speaking with Ms. Lezinsky?" asked Grant.

"Oh, I see. Yes, well she called me. I know her, of course, as I know all the parents of our students although some only by the names on their cheques. Anyhow, Dana called and asked if I could go see her. She was teary and sounded needy and frankly I wasn't keen to go because I'm not good at dealing with that sort of thing, but I knew Principal Johnson wouldn't have hesitated for a moment, so I went.

I'd never been to their home before, she told me you were there earlier, so I don't need to say anything about that."

"No, but how did you find Ms. Lezinsky?" At Judith's puzzled look Grant added, "In her person, how did she seem? I don't want to ask leading questions," he explained.

"I guess she was normal for the circumstances, I mean I didn't think about it. She looked terrible, but you saw her yourself. I'm not very good at describing people and I never wonder about how they're feeling or what they're thinking. Why would I?" Judith wasn't happy to hear that her voice sounded shaky.

She couldn't understand why she found Grant's questions disturbing. He seemed to sense this and told her to continue relating the conversation. Back on safe ground Judith regained her composure.

"Dana told me your autopsy revealed that Holly was pregnant. Dana has no idea who the father might be. Holly hung out with the boys in the trailer park, but she didn't show any interest in anyone particular, and Dana kept a watchful eye on her."

"Huh, not watchful enough!" interjected Suzanne.

Judith studied the woman's face for a moment trying to understand why she was so contemptuous. Suzanne herself was startlingly handsome with an athletic figure. She had a good job with the police and was now a detective. Judith thought Suzanne should be a much happier person than she appeared to be.

"Based on things she said, Dana is convinced that Holly was involved with some man. She spoke from intuition, not fact, because she didn't have any details," she added seeing the Grant was about to ask for more information.

"She also told me that she lied to you about Billy MacNeill and now wishes to recant her statement that gave him an alibi."

"Does she now!" exclaimed Grant, and Suzanne said:

"That's obstruction and it's a crime."

"She's a grieving mother, I doubt if you're going to convict or even charge her!" retorted Judith. She had little patience for Suzanne's negativity.

"Dana is quite definite that she doesn't think Billy MacNeill is responsible for Holly's pregnancy. However, now that her girl has been killed she couldn't care less about protecting him from whatever nonsense he's been up to."

"Hmm. Overall it's likely Ms. Lezinsky's judgement of her boyfriend is sound although plenty of women – and men – are often unpleasantly surprised at some of the things they learn about their mates.

Nevertheless we need to find Billy MacNeill and investigate whatever it is he was doing when Holly disappeared and again when she died."

"Do you know when that was?"

"The autopsy report suggests she was killed soon after she vanished. Again, we're waiting for the final results."

"Should we be discussing this with a civilian?" complained Suzanne. Grant ignored her comment and continued saying:

"After all, there's no evidence of any issues between Billy and Holly."

"Except for that fight they had at school a couple of days before she went missing," put in Judith.

"What fight?"

"Well, it was more of an argument, but he did yank her back when she walked away from him–" Suzanne interrupted her exclaiming:

"Why weren't the police informed about this incident?"

"I guess no one else saw what happened?" said Judith.

"But you did!"

"Oh, yes. I heard loud voices and looked out the window. From my office I can see the front driveway where he'd pulled up to get Holly from school. That happened quite often and her mother approved it. Anyhow, Holly got into the truck but a moment later she jumped back out again and started walking away. Billy MacNeill went after her and grabbing her arm he pulled her back to the truck and pushed her inside."

"That's kidnapping! Assault and battery at the very least!"

"No – and I already told all this to Dana Lezinsky – Holly's door didn't close properly so she opened it, moved whatever was in the way, and then closed it herself. Whatever it was that Billy said she accepted. If she'd wanted to get out the truck she could easily have done so. She could have run back into the school if she'd had any concerns, but she didn't."

"You should have mentioned this sooner," said Suzanne angrily.

"Why would I?"

"It's evidence."

"Evidence of what? I'm not privy to what was said, and I could have misinterpreted what I saw. I'm not a cop, it's not my job to make a report."

"It was your duty to tell us about Billy MacNeill."

"First off, I didn't even know you people existed so I could hardly tell you. Secondly, I didn't even remember this until today, and thirdly Holly's mother had alibied him. He was in the clear. The incident went right out of my mind."

"I can see how this all came about," said Grant in an effort to smooth things over but neither woman was admitting fault. To mollify his partner, he added:

"But it's disappointing to only be hearing about this incident now. We should have been informed about it sooner."

"Really? How about you should be doing your own job and I'll stick to mine. That's all I have to 'report' to you." Judith stood up, flushed and angry, and the officers were forced to go.

Chapter Fifteen

After the police left Judith remained on her feet. She started pacing back and forth, counting each step in a whisper:

"One, two, three, four, five, six, seven. One, two, three, four, five, six, seven."

Judith didn't realize Lila had come into the room until she said: "Oh! Is that an OCD thing? I know a bit about that."

"No, well at least not in my case. I don't have OCD. I mean I don't have to count but when I do it soothes me, calms me down."

"Why do you need calming down after a visit from the police? What happened?"

"He's so infuriating! and that woman hates me."

"No doubt she hates the fact that her Inspector Grant likes you. And if only he could see you now with your high colour and flashing eyes... Oops! I should probably have kept that thought to myself. But he is interested in you."

"No, he isn't. He was nicer than her, but as a matter of fact he was smarmy because he basically said the same thing she did, which was to complain about me not telling them about something I'd seen between Holly and that Billy MacNeill."

"Okay give me a second to untangle that sentence. Right, they're accusing you of withholding evidence."

"It's not evidence it's hearsay. Well, see I heard them yelling and oh forget about it. It wasn't the kidnapping Suzanne Mirteau tried to make it out to be. It was actually a nothing incident and I forgot all about it when I heard Dana had cleared Billy. Anyways, I did report this afternoon's conversation with Dana, and I guess the police will head over to her place now to confirm what she told me. I hope they treat her more kindly than they did me!"

"From my position on the sidelines I have to tell you I find all this fascinating. This is real drama like you see on TV. Although I'm crushed about a young girl being killed – have they confirmed yet if it's murder or suicide?"

"Not yet."

"Hmm, well that part is terribly sad – I did like Holly – but I have to confess the rest is pretty exciting stuff. Guess I lead an awfully boring life!"

"Oh, if only Pat hadn't gotten the flu, I wouldn't have had to deal with any of this. I'd be on the sidelines too. No, I wouldn't I'd be at home with my feet up enjoying my annual vacation."

"That's right! You were supposed to be off this week. But then you'd have missed all of this."

"I would be very pleased to give 'all of this' as you put it, a miss. Anyhow, since you're here you can give me some advice: do I go to the staff room to tell Marta and the rest of the coven about Holly's condition?"

"Oooh! Did I hear you call the teachers witches?"

"Oh God, I never meant to say that out loud. It's your fault, for some reason I can metaphorically-speaking let my hair down with you."

"I'll take that as a compliment! and yes, you should tell the Wicked Witch of the West about the pregnancy because it's going to get out and this way, with luck, you'll hear what the rumours are and then you can squash any innuendo."

"Good idea. Are you coming with me?"

"I wouldn't miss it!"

Chapter Sixteen

Judith and Lila headed to the staff-room to meet with the teachers who gathered there at the end of the working day to chat and unwind. Judith turned to Lila and asked:

"I know the Good Witch of the North was called Glinda but what was the name of the Wicked Witch of the West?"

"Marta," was Lila's quick comeback, then she snorted a laugh. That made both women dissolve into giggles.

"You're a snorter!" exclaimed Judith.

"Ha! I've been known to honk!"

They were still smiling when they entered the staff-room. The room was L-shaped with the doorway blocked from the main part by the cloakroom and row of lockers. What they heard took the smiles off their faces.

"Omigod this is awful! Play it again."

"Yes, replay that message and turn it up too."

Coming round the corner Judith and Lila looked at the circle of people who turned shocked faces towards them.

"Listen!" cried Jennifer, the young Maths teacher. She pointed to the answering machine and they all fell silent to hear the message.

"M-M-Miss Taylor, please, I need you to help me I don't know what to do and I'm so scared," wailed a young voice. "It's Beth, Beth Penner and I need to talk! I've got Holly's diary and I don't know what to do... do... do... about it. It's... it's awful." She broke into sobs and the rest of the message was her hiccupping voice stumbling over the words 'please help me' and 'I'm frightened'.

Everyone started speaking at the same time with questions like "what does she want?", and "what could be in Holly's diary?" and "why would Beth call Judith Taylor of all people?"

Lila and Judith moved closer to the machine and Lila pressed the Replay button. They waited in tense silence for the message to play again.

Listening to that tearful voice made Judith feel hot with embarrassment then goose-bumpy cold and nauseous but she closed her lips tight and inhaled through her nose to slow her breathing. She needed to calm down and think but her finger hovered over the Delete button and she really wanted to press down hard.

Chapter Seventeen

"The police will want to know about this!" declared Marta.

Her voice seems to break the spell Judith has been under. She desperately wants to ignore the message but too many people have heard it and she is forced to act.

"Yes, you're right, for sure I must contact them right away. This diary could provide vital evidence, it might tell us who..."

"That's right," picked up Lila. "We actually came to the staff-room to share the news Judith had from Dana Lezinsky, Holly's mother. The police told her that Holly was pregnant when she died."

Other than a collective gasp of "Pregnant!" no one spoke until Marta said to Judith:

"But that doesn't explain why it's you Beth wants to talk to."

"I have no idea either. I mean, of course I know Beth, but she's never wanted to confide in me before."

"I can believe that," an unidentified voice muttered. Judith suspected it was Xiao, he was always very critical of everyone, and he was Marta's puppet.

"That doesn't matter, Judith," said Noel eagerly, "What's important is that you get over to Beth's place right away. I'll drive you. I know where she lives because I took her and Holly home after a late rehearsal once. We should go now; we shouldn't waste any time."

"No, we should leave it to the police. They've made it crystal clear they don't want civilians butting in."

"But Beth called YOU, not the police. What if she won't talk to them?" said one person.

"Right! What if it's the police she's afraid of?" exclaimed another and everyone joined in to agree.

"When did this phone message come in?" asked Judith.

"It must be fifteen or twenty minutes ago now. We've listened to it a couple of times and as new people came in, as you did, we listened again."

"Well, the police ought to be told." Judith knows she's stalling but she's struggling against the opinions of everyone crowding round her.

"Look, I'll go with you and Noel," offered Lila so Judith had to agree.

"Hurry up," urged Noel. "I don't think there's any time to lose."

Chapter Eighteen

The drive to Beth Penner's home took about thirty minutes and Judith spent that time struggling with her feelings. She desperately wanted to maintain her usual arms-length stance but knew she no longer could.

Forced to deputize for Principal Johnson meant she was being pushed into liaising with the bereaved family, the friends, police, coworkers, and now students, as well.

She must deal with this phone message. Beth sounds very clingy and is demanding attention that Judith is loathe to give. But she knows she can't abandon the girl, even though she wants to. Silently she berates herself for even thinking such a thing. Yet it's true. Nobody cares that I didn't ask for this!

Lila and Noel have both been talking while all these thoughts were chasing around in Judith's head. She hasn't been paying attention, and didn't even realize that the three of them left the school without their coats and it's cold out. Judith doesn't even have her purse or her phone. Ever since she heard Beth's message on the answering machine it's like she's been cocooned with her own thoughts. Thoughts racing through her mind like a hamster exercising in its wheel.

The Penner's house is a white brick bungalow with blue shutters matching the colour of the garage door. They pull into the empty driveway and hurry out of the car to the ring the doorbell. They can hear it chime but no one answers. They ring again and knock harder but still no answer. Noel lifts the flap of the letter box and calls "Hello? Beth? Hello?" however there's no reply.

"Does her mother work? Would she go there?" asked Lila.

"Her mother passed away, it's only Beth – no brothers or sisters – and her Dad. He'll be at work. I don't have his number, but I'll have it on file at the school. We should go back and I'll phone him."

"No!" said Noel. "No point worrying him until we know more. We should wait here for a while."

Lila shivered and in that moment Judith felt the cold as well.

"I don't want to hang around here. It's cold–"

"Not in the car it isn't, we can wait in there," pleaded Noel, but the women wanted to leave.

The empty house was a letdown after their rush to get there, but Judith was secretly pleased, it felt like a reprieve.

Chapter Nineteen

"Judith why would Beth phone you for help?" asked Noel as they headed back to the school.

Judith wasn't interested in cars but enjoyed the comfort of the luxurious vehicle he drove. The heat was blasting out the vents and the car was even equipped with seat warmers. She felt far more relaxed now that she was warm and the confrontation with Beth averted. For the time being, at least.

"I don't know why she would."

"Yeah, well no offence but you're not exactly the warm-and-cuddly type. You're not very maternal."

"Noel, I'd be offended if you said I was that type!" laughed Judith. "But no, you're right, it doesn't make sense."

"It's because you're not the motherly sort," said Lila from the backseat. "I mean, ever since her mother died there will have been relatives, neighbours, and other women hanging around wanting to smother her in hugs and urging her to cry and 'let it out'. Hearing enough stuff like that would turn any sensitive child off. Then there's you, somebody who isn't going to fuss her and will listen instead of saying 'don't think about that, put it right out of your mind'. Does that make sense?"

"Actually, it makes a lot of sense to me," said Noel. "Knowing that someone will give you an honest, straightforward answer is a comfort. Too many people tell you what they think you want to hear, or what they think you should hear. They try to protect you from the truth and that can be so frustrating."

Judith and Lila exchanged a look at Noel's comment, each wondering what particular memory he was recalling.

"But still, there must be more to it than just that. Think Judith! what have you and Beth talked about in the last while?"

Judith breathed out a gusty breath saying she'd have to cast her mind back. She definitely had spoken to Beth when they first discovered Holly was missing. In fact, since Beth was Holly's best friend she'd been questioned by the police and Judith had sat in on the interview as the Appropriate Adult. That happened about a week ago and Judith had been preoccupied with her own discomfort. She knew that she wasn't good with people and their emotional messes.

"I was called to accompany her when Holly went missing and the police came to the school. I didn't want to go to the interview because I was busy with my own work. I was trying to get most of my new year set-up completed since I was taking my vacation and didn't want to come back and have to hustle. But for some reason, if I'm remembering it right, there was an unavoidable Trustee meeting, Pat Johnson couldn't be present so she asked me to sit in.

As it turned out it didn't take long. Beth had very little to say to the two policemen – two different ones than now – she could only tell them when she'd last seen Holly and if Holly had said anything about going somewhere, or if she'd fought with her mother, or anything like that.

I got the impression that the police believed Holly had left of her own free will. I didn't get any sense of real worry from Beth or urgency from the police, although looking back there should have been."

"Hindsight, yadda-yadda."

"True."

"Had Holly run away before? Did she have a reputation for doing so? or for staying away overnight?" asked Lila.

"No!" Noel said loudly. "Holly wasn't like that at all, not a bit. She was a really sweet girl, very tenderhearted and kind. A gentle soul."

Again, Lila and Judith exchanged looks. This wasn't the Holly they knew, and Noel's sentimentality came as a surprise. Judith remembered that Annalise claimed he'd called her a 'gentle soul' as well. Was it some sort of pick-up line? Surely not, Holly was just a child.

"Well, you saw a lot of her with the play and everything so I'm sure you knew here much better than we did," answered Lila.

Noel dismissed that idea saying: "I wouldn't say I knew her that well," then qualified his answer by adding: "but I probably did see another side to her."

Chapter Twenty

"Where could Beth be? All the children left school ages ago," wondered Judith.

"Do you think she's gone out for dinner with her father?" asked Lila.

Noel had left his car running at the school's front driveway – a no-no in the 'No Idling' zone – but said he'd only be a moment running up the steps to grab his coat and briefcase. The women made their way to the principal's office and sat down to discuss this new turn of events.

"That's possible, or when you think about it she could be anywhere at this time of year: shopping or out at another friend's place."

"So, you think worrying about her is premature."

"Oh, probably but.." Judith hesitated a moment to think about this. Was it normal to worry about the whereabouts of a young teen? Judith didn't know but Beth was obviously in distress. Unless that was teen drama? "I have to say I don't know. What do you think?" she asked Lila.

"You should tell the police about the message left on the answering machine, and explain that you tried to get in touch with Beth but there was no one at her home."

"And then leave it in their hands! Yes, that's a good idea." Judith hoped she didn't sound too eager but Lila was following her own train of thought:

"Or we could go back to Beth's place later? We could have a meal and then drop by again just to be sure."

"No, if we bring in the police we have to leave them to do their job. Anything else would be interfering. Besides, they've got the resources."

Lila seemed doubtful but didn't argue, instead she replied:

"You could ask them to let you know what they find out. Beth called you so it's only natural you'd want to know that the girl's okay."

"Yes, I could ask them to do that. Not sure if they will tell me but I can ask."

"Okay then, let's get the announcement out about tomorrow's meeting."

"Good idea. I honestly don't know if anyone will show up. Do we want the teachers to attend?"

"No, but they might want to do so. How about we tell them a meeting is scheduled but say that attendance isn't mandatory."

"Yes, that's good. Also, I'm not planning on serving anything, so we'd better let them know that."

"Right, they might expect coffee."

"Oh, our parents expect much more than that! Whenever we have a meeting the girl's get to practise their baking skills, laying out trays, and serving. It's always quite the affair. Of course, we usually ask the parents to RSVP so we know the numbers and can cater accordingly."

"Something to look forward to at some future date!"

"Yes, it is always nicely done. Now if we make it six o'clock that will give everyone the opportunity to eat early or go out afterwards. So, we could say something like 'December 21 at 6:00 pm an informal meeting at the school for parents with questions about recent events. RSVP not required and no food or drink will be served.' How does that sound?"

"Yes, it covers everything. Same deal as before: you email and I text?"

"You got it."

"This won't take us long and then we can go get a bite to eat."

"Oh, not me, no but thanks anyhow. I've still got some work to do here, things I was planning to get on with when I got the call from Dana Lezinsky."

Lila looked mildly disappointed but only commented: "That seems like ages ago!"

"Only a few hours but yes, a lot has happened since then. I'll walk to the staff room with you to grab my coat as well. That'll save me a trip when I leave."

"Remember and make sure you do call the police – I think it's important and you don't want to give them any reason to complain."

"I agree! and I'll call for sure. I'm a bit concerned about Beth myself, I mean that phone message was..."

"Yes, it was definitely a cry for help."

Chapter Twenty-One

"Well, that was easier than I expected," thought Judith, smiling to herself. She reached Grant's voicemail when she called so was able to leave a message and avoid having a conversation. "Now I can get back to doing my real job."

Opening her laptop to get to work on her books Judith ignored the first guilty twinge but eventually the nagging of her conscience was too distracting. Against her instincts she picked up the business card again and looked for a main phone number to the police station. Sighing heavily, she dialled the number.

"Edgemont Police Station is this an emergency?"

"Uh no, no it isn't but it's important, well it is to me... Sorry I sound ridiculous..."

"Go ahead and explain, ma'am," said the dispatcher's bored-sounding voice.

"My name is Judith Taylor and I work at Edgemont School for Girls. One of our students phoned and left a tearful message on our answering machine and she sounded frightened by something. I've been unable to get hold of her since. I don't know her cellphone number..." Judith paused a moment to jot down a reminder to make a directory of all student's cellphone numbers, "but I went by her house and there was no one home."

"What time was this phone message left, and what's the name of the girl?"

"I'm not sure what time, hmm... it was about 3:30 to 4:00? Students left early today. We aren't having regular classes because of our other student, Holly Lezinsky, who was found dead after being missing a week.

I guess that's why I'm concerned about Beth, her full name is Bethany Penner, in case something's happened. Also, her message says she's scared but not why she's scared."

"I'm initiating a call out for the girl right now. You say there's a connection to the Holly Lezinsky case?"

"The two of them are... um, were, best friends and Beth claims she's got Holly's diary but I'm not sure if that's important. Detectives Grant and Mirteau have been here twice talking to me and the rest of the staff so I called them first but couldn't get hold of them, I had to leave a message. I don't know when Detective Grant will get it and Beth is only fourteen so..."

"You're doing the right thing Ms. Taylor. We'll start searching for the girl, and someone will follow up with you tonight or tomorrow."

"Thank you, I appreciate that. I don't like to fuss or waste time but..."

"Not at all, we appreciate your concern. Thanks again, good-bye."

After ending the call Judith found she was unable to return to her work because now she couldn't stop wondering, even worrying, about Beth. For a moment she considered calling Lila to give her an update but decided that would be intruding since Lila said she was going out for a meal. They could catch up tomorrow.

Judith switched off her computer, gathered up her belongings, and put on her coat. She didn't turn out any lights since the school custodian would be in sometime later to check up and would deal with the lights and the heating then. As she approached the front door she was clearly outlined against the darkness outside. She hesitated a moment with an eerie feeling that she was being watched.

She was.

Wrongly, she decided she was being fanciful and so she shrugged it off and locked up, walking at a fast pace across to the parking lot and into the safe haven of her car.

Until a body smashed against the driver's side door, grabbing at the door handle. Judith had locked that the moment she got in so the attacker was stymied but he, for she could see it was a man, started pounding on the window and yelling obscenities and threats. She pushed away from the door, fright turning to terror. Frozen in fear while this wild-eyed, raging and ranting man fought to get into her car.

In a split-second Judith recovered enough to blast the horn, over and over again, which startled the man into falling back from the vehicle. She sped away with her hands in a painful grip on the steering-wheel and her breath coming in gasps.

From what she could see and from what he'd said she figured that must have been Billy MacNeill. Complaining about what she'd said about him and Holly to his wife – although Judith knew he wasn't married to Dana – and vowing to get even with... well, she didn't need to remind herself about the insults.

Her first burst of fearful emotion soon gave way to anger. "How dare he! He has no right..." she was outraged and her thoughts were a bit jumbled.

Judith realized the man, Billy MacNeill, had been very drunk and most likely she hadn't been in any danger. She figured he'd have shouted abuse in the hopes of making her cry. She didn't need to be afraid of him. The fact that he'd come to the school meant it was doubtful he knew where she lived.

"Oh, of course he doesn't know that. I bet he doesn't even know my surname." She exclaimed, exasperated with herself. "Get home and make a cup of tea or better yet, a hot chocolate. The sugar will help. Then call the police. No, I've already got a call in to the police, so I'll just wait until Grant phones me back. Billy MacNeill will not be a problem, I won't allow it!" she declared.

Chapter Twenty-Two

In the wintertime especially, Judith liked that her building had underground parking. Her spot was close to the inside door and she could see the overhead garage door in her rear-view mirror. She always watched to make sure no one sneaked in while she was waiting for it to close.

When a new building manager had told her she'd have to change parking spots she'd flat out refused. He tried to argue claiming he needed that space for crews coming in to work on the building but she suspected he wanted it for his own car. She told him it was a safety issue for her and that she was prepared to take it up with owner of the building. That hadn't been necessary because she heard no more about it, and that manager hadn't lasted too long.

Once she was locked inside her own apartment, feeling a little sheepish at how she'd almost run from her car to the door, Judith wanted to review the incident and get it all straight in her mind. Lila had added her contact info to Judith's cellphone so Judith called to update her on the Billy MacNeill incident.

"Omigod that must have been so scary!"

"It was. I mean I'm locking the front door of the school, it's quiet and dark, nobody's around but you know I had this creepy feeling that someone was watching me. And I'm not imagining that in light of what happened, I did feel something was dodgy. Anyhow, turns out I was being watched by Billy MacNeill of all people."

"What did he say?"

"It's hard to recall exactly... he was hollering and cursing and it was obvious he was very drunk. I mean, too drunk to be a problem because if I'd had to I could easily have outrun him and I'm not a runner! but when he suddenly loomed up beside the car door and started pounding on the windows, yeah he startled me and I was frightened."

"I would have peed my pants."

Judith laughed at Lila saying: "You'd have been out of your car with your fists up, I know you've got a fiery temper!"

"I prefer to call myself 'feisty', it's the Italian way. So, what did Grant say when you told him?"

"I haven't talked to him yet."

"You've got to let him know; I'm positive you'll find he's very concerned. This might be important evidence and your personal safety might be on the line."

"I don't think that's true, MacNeill was acting out in a stupid-drunk way. But I did call Grant and left a message for him to call me back."

"Well then I won't keep you on the phone. Thanks for letting me know and Judith if you start feeling scared or anything on your own call me. I can come over there or you can come over here."

"Thanks, that's nice of you, but I'll be fine, and I'll see you at school tomorrow."

They said their goodbyes and hung up. When the phone rang shortly after Judith expected it to be Grant but instead if was Annalise calling.

"You don't mind me phoning you at home, do you Judith?"

"Well, actually–"

"I got your number from Noel, he's got a directory of all the staff. He's so organized."

"I don't mind so long as you make it quick, Annalise. I've had a very long day already." Judith felt she'd already put up with enough of Annalise's dithering when the younger woman had visited the school. Now she just wanted her to get to the point.

"Oh! Well, that's easy because it's a simple request. My in-laws-to-be asked me to call and invite you to tea tomorrow. At their home."

"Why?"

"Why? Oh, I expect they want to pick your brains about what's going on with the murder and everything. They like to get the facts firsthand and of course as you're acting on Pat Johnson's behalf you're the man-of-the-hour, so to speak," she ended with a giggle.

"Well, that's very kind but my time isn't my own right now so I can't be sure if I'll even be free in the afternoon."

"Oh, you don't have to wait until four o'clock, in fact they'd rather have you come early. The sooner the better, actually. They'll be home all day and since Cook will be baking the goodies bright and early just drop by as soon as you can. They'll be waiting."

Judith couldn't see any way out of the invitation. She knew Pat Johnson would want her to accept because Eleanor Frampton did so much for the school financially. The woman's support meant funding came from her social circle as well.

Also, since Judith wasn't going to be attending Noel's birthday and Christmas party this was her chance to see the house. "It is an estate after all," she thought to herself, "and no doubt worth seeing 'how the 1% live'!" Aloud she said:

"Well. please pass on my thanks, Annalise and say I'll be delighted to take tea as early in the day as I can manage."

"Oooh that's wonderful news. We'll see you tomorrow, then. Byeeeee."

Judith considered her wardrobe while wondering what to wear for the appointment then decided she'd go ahead with the outfit she'd already planned on. She didn't feel obliged to dress up, in fact she was a bit resentful at having to attend at all. She was interested in seeing their home but she didn't like being summoned, it made her feel imposed upon.

"On the other hand," she thought, "I can use it as a practice run for seeing the parents at tomorrow night's meeting."

She meant it when she'd told Annalise that it had been a long day and she felt like relaxing in hot bubble-bath. She took her cellphone with her in the bathroom but Grant never did return her call.

Chapter Twenty-Three

Why am I so stiff today?" wondered Judith speaking out loud although she was alone. She always spoke to herself; she hummed and sang out loud as well.

Each morning she counted her way through twenty-five toe touches but today she didn't make contact until attempt number four. She performed this routine in the shower figuring that if she lost her balance and fell the distance wouldn't be far. She was lucky that her bathtub/shower combo had proper doors instead of a shower-curtain.

The toe touching was to stretch. Judith didn't participate in any formal kind of exercise – no sports teams, jogging, or gym membership – but she did enjoy a good walk.

Year-round, so long as the weather was dry, she walked to work each day. Snowfall didn't deter her, but rain did. Walking in the rain made her feel very stupid, worrying that people would think she was 'too dumb to come in out of the rain'. The fact that there was no one to think that didn't matter – Judith herself would think that.

"I expect I'm achy because I tossed and turned so much last night. That idiot Billy MacNeill gave me quite a scare and I guess I'm feeling the aftermath of that. Also, I've had Beth on my mind, she's a worry; and my trip out of school – to Dana Lezinsky's home – was unusual. Then I got thinking about how much I enjoy Lila's company, and after that I rehashed that argument with Grant. Of course, I always think of much better comebacks when I'm writing the script! He never did call me back so it's just as well I called the police station main number too.

I hope I haven't gotten Beth into trouble with her father, I'm sure things are difficult for both of them with no mother in the house. And then that surprise call from Annalise inviting me, as if I have a choice! to join her at the Larkin house to 'drink a cup of tea and discuss the unfortunate situation'. How can she think of the murder as an 'unfortunate situation'? Unless she means the cancellation of the play? that would make her even more shallow! but it could be she's concerned after all the time and hard work Noel put into it. I don't know. With all this going around in my head it's a wonder I got any sleep at all.

Today's forecast is rain turning to snow and that overcast sky looks ready to fulfill it. Ugh, I hate driving in sleet but it's better than walking in it. It will be best if I take the car all week anyways in case I get called out in addition to this tea drinking with the school's most generous supporters. I expect Beth has turned up by now, so I'll have to go out to her home again if she asks."

Walking down the stairs to the parking garage Judith at the odd twinge of pain. "Maybe I've got a touch of this flu bug that's going around? If so, at least it won't be severe since I've had my shot." She didn't realize that when she violently jerked her body away from the car door last night that she wrenched a few muscles. These minor aches would plague her all day.

Judith drove slowly since the promised precipitation arrived and made the roads slick. Fortunately, there was very little traffic. This close to Christmas meant the shoppers would be out in force but both malls were in the opposite direction from where she was headed.

There were several intersections to get through and she kept an eye on the pedestrians' WALK/DON'T WALK signal to get a warning when the light was about to turn red. The actual driving was okay but stopping could be a challenge under these conditions.

As she got near to the school she noticed the car behind was following too closely, especially in this weather. It didn't have its headlights on so she couldn't get a good look but it appeared to be a dark-coloured car that was bigger than hers. She changed lanes to allow the driver room to pass but instead he – or she – moved into the lane behind her and stayed right there whether she sped up or slowed down.

Judith was getting annoyed, the road conditions required concentration and she couldn't keep looking in her rear-view mirror. What was the other driver doing? Were they sticking close because they couldn't see very well themselves? they might not realize their lights weren't on. Regardless, it was annoying to have someone tailgating her, she was concerned about being rear-ended.

With relief she spotted the school and was almost at its driveway when the car behind roared to life and clipped her left bumper as it raced past.

Judith's car began to spin out of control heading towards the wall of old trees that lined the road. Without thinking about it she threw the car into neutral and was able to slow it down enough to regain control. Popping it into a low gear she managed to drive into the skid and straighten out. Her heart was pounding, and her chest heaved with shallow breaths, but she was okay, and the car was still running.

"That stupid, stupid person driving so dangerously," she thought. "What a lousy way to start my day!"

It didn't occur to her that the near-crash wasn't accidental.

Steering onto the school grounds she spotted an unfamiliar sports-car parked in the lot and suspected it belonged to Suzanne Mirteau.

"A second lousy thing to ruin my day. If it turns out that bad things do come in threes I'm done for," Judith grumbled.

Chapter Twenty-Four

The office staff usually got to work before the teachers arrived but today Marta and a few cohorts were already at the school, waiting. Judith gave Marta's triumphant expression a puzzled look before noticing the grim faces on Grant and Suzanne.

"What's going on?" she asked, while nudging her way past Joanna, Jennifer, and Xiao, and walking up to the detectives.

"Let's take this into your office, Ms. Taylor. It's an informal interview but still best done without interruptions."

Grant didn't look towards Marta but Judith felt they all knew exactly what he meant. Without a word she marched to the principal's office, hung up her coat behind the door and sat in Pat's chair after putting her purse and briefcase on the credenza. The silence extended until Suzanne broke it with an accusation:

"You've withheld evidence from the police again!"

"No I haven't!" retorted Judith.

"Ms. Smith told us all about a phone message that was left to you on the answering machine. A message from a frightened, crying girl who claimed she had some evidence from the victim and you didn't tell us. And you—"

"I did I–" but Suzanne didn't let Judith interrupt, she was angry and continued:

"Went off playing detective! Instead of contacting us immediately you and your pals drove out to see this girl Bethany Penner on your own. Why? Do you think you know better than us? Do you think you're smarter than the dumb cops? is that it?" She was working herself up and Judith wondered how much of this tirade could be heard through the office door. She didn't doubt for a moment that Marta and the other teachers would be lurking nearby.

Judith refused to engage in a noisy argument. She turned her attention to Grant who gestured to Suzanne to stop. Judith took that opportunity to say:

"Several of the teachers urged me not to contact the police until I spoke to Beth in case she was afraid because of something she'd done or for some other reason, whatever it might be, that she didn't want the police involved. However, if you check at the police station, you'll find that I did call. I called there after I couldn't get hold of you," she held Grant's gaze adding, "The phone message was to me, that's correct, and so I responded to it. I wanted to see Beth to find out what she needed from me. If there was any reason to call the police after I learned what she had to say I would have done so."

"That's not up to you!"

Judith continued speaking to Grant as if Suzanne hadn't said a word.

"Since I was unable to reach Beth, and because I was concerned about her phone-call to me, I did leave a message for you. When you didn't phone me back I called the station and they took my report over the phone. There was an incident after that which I was going to tell you when you returned my call but... you didn't."

Grant sat up looking concerned: "What incident?"

"A man tried to attack me when I left the school last night. He was waiting in the parking lot here-—"

"Stop trying to deflect us with this fabrication!" exclaimed Suzanne.

"Who, to the best of my knowledge, was Billy MacNeill. Drunk, but coherent enough for me to know he was very angry and making wild accusations."

"You know MacNeill?"

"I've seen him from a distance on those occasions when he drove to the school to pick up Holly. Last night I thought I recognized him and also because of what he said."

Suzanne threw up her hands and fell back into a chair. She crossed her arms and legs, swinging one of them, and looking like a petulant child furious at being ignored. Judith and Grant continued to ignore her. He said,

"I'll need a full statement with all those details – you will press charges, won't you?"

"That depends. I don't want to add to Dana Lezinsky's troubles. She might have changed her mind and be willing to forgive him and take him back. If that's the case, I won't upset her further.

However, that man has no right to go around scaring people just because he can't control his temper or handle his drink. I hope you, or if not you some officer, shakes him up a bit. Not actually shaking of course but let him know that his behaviour has been noted as part of the official record or whatever you call it."

"Any other personal chores we can attend to for you?" Suzanne was sarcastic and snarky. Grant shook his head and told Judith not to worry, the incident would be logged and investigated. He glanced back at Suzanne and added that he would take care of it himself.

"Actually there is something else. We've called an impromptu parents' meeting for this evening and it would be great to have a police spokesperson to answer their questions. It's very last minute, I know, and it could be that no parents actually do show up but it would help us and it would look good for the police, too."

Suzanne got up and left the room without answering.

Judith felt herself relaxing a bit now that she and Grant were alone. He had such a calm manner whereas Suzanne seemed to buzz with negative energy. It crackled off her. Without considering her words beforehand Judith blurted out: "You two do make an odd couple."

Grant gave a slight smile saying: "That's because we aren't a 'couple'. We're work-mates and yes, we have different attitudes and different ways of looking at things, but that helps each of us get a broader viewpoint. To be honest though I've never seen my partner act with such aggression. I can only think it's because the victim was so young and with the holidays so close, well... it's a heartbreaking situation."

"I thought the police had to put their feelings aside."

"Oh we have to and we do, otherwise we couldn't work our job. But that doesn't mean we don't feel it, only that we have to compartmentalize in order to get on with it. We have feelings too, you know."

"I didn't mean to offend you."

"You didn't, and I'm sorry if I made it sound like you had. Actually, I am feeling a bit prickly myself, so I guess this case it getting to everyone."

"Either that or Suzanne is rubbing off on you."

The smile left his face and she realized it wasn't much of a joke.

"I'll talk to my boss about this meeting with the parents, there's very little we're able to share at this time so I don't know how worthwhile it would be."

Judith shrugged and said if he or anyone could make it great but not to worry. As Grant turned to go he said he hoped she would get in touch with Ms. Lezinsky soon and for Judith to let him know what she'd decided regarding pressing charges against Billy MacNeill.

"I'll leave you a message with my answer, you won't need to call me back."

Grant looked like he wanted to reply to that remark but after a pause he nodded and left the office.

Judith watched when the two of them appeared outside the window. The principal's office gave a better view of the front area than her office did. She briefly wondered how 'Chatterbox Cindy' was managing on her own at their shared room in the library. Judith figured she'd be spending most of her time in the staff-room.

Grant and Suzanne were arguing about something. Their body language showed that both were angry and neither was trying to placate the other. Judith wondered what it was all about. With the windows closed to the December cold she couldn't hear a thing.

Once the police drove away Judith should have settled down to work but she felt unable to do so. She blamed it on her poor sleep from last night, her overall acheyness, and the lack of physical exercise recently. That and the constant bickering with the police combined to make her cranky and restless.

She decided to put her things away in the staff cloakroom and fetch a coffee, hoping to find Lila in one of those locations so she could catch her up on the news.

Chapter Twenty-Five

Lila was in the hallway hurrying towards Principal Johnson's office.

"I was just coming to look for you," began Judith but Lila cut her off whispering:

"Don't talk, super-cute guy who is SO mad coming right up behind me." She broke off as a deep voice called out:

"I want to see this Judith Taylor woman right now!"

The man, wearing a hi-vis vest over work clothes and safety boots, appeared beside Lila, and he was very angry.

And yes, he was also handsome in a rugged, outdoorsy way with his dark-red hair and bright brown eyes, an unusual combination. But Judith brushed that thought aside. He was a big man and in this mood he was intimidating. She lifted her chin stating:

"I am Judith Taylor and you had better come into my office and explain your business in our school." She signalled to Lila to join them.

Once in the office, with Judith seated behind her desk and Lila standing by the door, the man's anger turned to anxiety. He clutched his head in both hands and gasped out:

"I am frantic with worry. I don't know what's going on around here, but my little girl is missing." Judith met Lila's eyes and saw recognition there.

Lila guided Brian Penner, both women realizing that this was Beth's father, into a chair and sat down herself beside him. Judith came round from her desk and perched on the edge. This more intimate arrangement seemed to comfort the man.

"Mr. Penner, we are both terribly sorry to hear this about Beth. We went to your home looking for her yesterday right after school. No one was in and we thought the two of you had gone out. However, Beth is very young, so I called the police station to report our concern. You see, Beth left a tearful message on the school's answering machine, and we haven't heard from her or been able to get hold of her since."

"What message?"

"She said she had found her friend Holly's diary and something in it upset her very much because she was crying and saying she was scared."

"Scared? Scared of what?"

"That's all she said. You do know about Holly Lezinsky, right?"

"Holly's missing, yeah I heard all about it from Bethany, she's been beside herself."

"Oh Mr. Penner--"

"Brian."

"Brian, thank you, I'm afraid that Holly has been found dead by the police."

"No! Oh no, not Holly! Oh, poor Beth. Now she'll be devastated. But the police never said a word to me. I spoke to a woman called um, Suzie? I've got her card here somewhere." As he searched his pockets Judith and Lila again exchanged a look.

"Was the policewoman's name Suzanne Mirteau?"

"Yeah! that's it, I remember she had a French name."

"What exactly did Detective Mirteau tell you?"

"She said that Bethany would be here at school with you, that my daughter went home with you yesterday. I guess that sorta makes sense since she'd been upset about Holly missing and now, knowing she died, but I mean, who are you? and what are you to Bethany?" He looked puzzled but Judith could sense his anger simmering below this surface calm.

"Mr... Brian, I have no idea why Detective Mirteau would say that. I have never taken a student home with me and if, for some unimaginable reason, I ever feel called upon to do so the first thing I'd do is notify her family. I'm the school Bursar and I have very little to do with Beth or any of the students. I know who the girls are – for the most part – but I deal with the parents. And the bureaucracy."

"Then why did Bethany try to get hold of you? and why was she crying?"

"That's what we're all wondering. Lila here, who is the school Nurse, and I have been trying to figure that out." All of a sudden he jumped up saying:

"I'm wasting time sitting and talking with you. It isn't doing any good. I've got to find her. I need to know what the police are doing. If they think she's here at school with you then they won't be out looking for her. I'm going back to the station."

"I will call your home and will keep trying. Does Beth have a cellphone?"

He thrust his own phone at her saying: "I don't remember the number but it's in here." Lila took the phone from him and quickly found the number which she wrote down.

"We'll both keep trying to get hold of Beth all day. Tell the police to let the school know when they have news. Actually, I'm putting Judith's number into your phone – that will be much faster since you'll get through right away. I don't want to hold you up now but try to think of the names of friends Beth might be staying with because the police will want that information."

"I always thought Holly was her only friend. They've been best friends for years. I never saw any other girls come by the home or heard them mention meeting up with anyone else. I've gotta find Bethany, she needs me, and I wasn't there for her."

"Brian, we're having an informal meeting with parents tonight and you might want to come to see if anyone knows anything or, if you can't make it we'll ask on your behalf. With it being last-minute and, of course, a busy time of year we might not get much of a turnout but nevertheless..."

"Yes, unless the police need me I'll be there. There was a text, I guess, but I don't remember."

"It's scheduled for six o'clock here."

The two women walked with him to the entrance, giving assurances that they would all keep in touch. Judith told Brian that at school Beth preferred to be called 'Beth', not Bethany, so that's how her classmates and their families would know her. He said he'd try to remember that, then walked away.

It was too cold to stand outside but they watched from the vestibule as he drove off in his pick-up truck. It was snowing now, and the lawn had a covering of white. The school had hired a landscaping firm to create a drive-through by cutting an arc from the road to the front entrance and back to the road again. Alumnae had protested the change, but it prevented the girls from ruining the grass, in addition to being much safer for pick-ups and drop-offs to happen off the road and on school property.

"Judith why are there so many hot-looking men involved in this case? Teacher, Cop, Parent... wow!"

"Gee Lila, I was thinking about what that poor man is going through, not rating him on a 'hotness scale'." said Judith.

"How could you not be? Oh well, stick with me and you'll catch on, kid. So far as Beth is concerned we need to keep thinking positive thoughts and hope for the best," replied Lila.

"Why did you give him my phone number?"

"Because I couldn't give him mine – I'm married."

Chapter Twenty-Six

Lila's statement was a shocker but before Judith could speak Noel came up to them in the foyer to say a ton of messages were piling up on the answering machine.

"I answered one of them because the caller was the mother of one of my girls but boy was that a mistake! I couldn't get her off the line even though all I said, over and over, was 'we don't know, the police haven't said, I have no idea' – it was so frustrating. I let the rest pile up. Anyhow, Judith I did want to talk to you..." his voice trailed off as he looked at Lila. She took the hint saying:

"I'll head to the staff-room now and see it I can't make some headway with those messages," and gave Judith a wink.

Judith had never cared for Noel's affectation of calling his students 'his girls' but she didn't comment on that, she wanted to hear what he had to say. He took her by the arm and pulled her in close so he could speak in a low voice.

"I want to let you know that there's quite a bit of back-biting going on amongst the teachers and it's directed at you. The main complaint seems to be that Pat Johnson should have put Marta in charge, not you, since you aren't even a teacher. Also, that phone message..."

Judith waited for more then realized that was it. She sighed inside thinking Noel was very young after all. This Christmas Day was either his 26th or 27th birthday, she wasn't sure which. The fact that his and Holly's birthdays were only days apart, and that each of them had Christmas-related names, had been yet another bond between the two of them.

"Noel, understand that I do not care what the teachers think. The decision was made, and they must abide by it, regardless of their opinion. I know I'm not a popular person, that's part of the reason why Pat knows she can trust me: I won't play favourites, in fact I won't play games of any kind."

"Nor should you! I totally agree with everything you're saying! but I thought it was important that you know what's going on. Boy, I wish I had your guts! I care way too much about what people think about me," he said with a half-laugh.

"Why? You've got it all, Noel. You're great at your job, you're a good-looking man, your family is well-off, you've got a beautiful fiancee, and you're a nice guy to boot!"

"Aww, it's so kind of you to say all that! You're right, I'm lucky in so many ways. I should be more self-confident."

"That's right. We've only got to get through the next few days and everything will be back to normal when we return in the new year."

"Well, not everything." said Noel with a sigh, looking forlorn. Judith wasn't sure if he meant Holly or his play. She decided not to ask. For such a handsome, manly-looking man Noel Larkin could be quite needy.

"I'm sure that's a tactic that works very well with plenty of women," she thought, "but not with me."

Since Judith didn't react Noel settled for giving a sad little smile saying:

"You're right, of course. Somebody's stirring things up. It will be Marta behind it all but she's got plenty of acolytes to do her bidding while her hands stay clean. I thought you should know. Friends need to stick together." He moved away then turned back saying:

"I hear you're having a goss with my ladies today?" adding, when Judith looked puzzled, "A gossip, 'tea and scandal' with my mother, auntie, and Annalise," he explained.

"Oh right, yes. Feels like a command performance," Judith replied, wondering if he'd named the women in order of importance to him.

"Not that bad, surely!" Noel laughed.

"Actually, I was thinking it will be like a trial run for tonight. Did anyone tell you about the parents' meeting we're having? Teachers aren't required to attend but of course can if they want, if you want. We're not serving any food or drink so we figure no one will stay too long!"

"What's the agenda?"

"Nothing formal, a Q and A except we won't have very many answers! No doubt it will turn into a venting session. I'm not expecting to get much of a turn-out. It's short notice and it's such a busy time with social, shopping, and family stuff.

Unfortunately, the ones most likely to show up will be those people who love to hear themselves talk. Wow, I'm really not selling it, am I?"

Noel laughed and told her to definitely take the opportunity of her daytime visit with his family to practise for her nighttime meeting with the parents saying:

"The idea will be to pump you for inside information, politely of course! although I'm sure my ears will be burning, too!" He gave a little wave and this time did walk away.

Judith hadn't been looking forward to the 'tea party', even less so now that she knew she'd be grilled. It annoyed her so she decided:

"Now I'm just in the mood for a chat with Suzanne."

Chapter Twenty-Seven

Judith returned to her office to make the call but before doing so tried both of Beth's numbers again. She'd left a message at each earlier so didn't bother doing so again.

Picking up Grant's business card she entered his cell number into her contacts. Easier than looking it up each time. When he picked up, she immediately launched into her attack:

"I've just had Beth Penner's father in here accusing me of abducting his daughter because – apparently – that's what you detectives told him happened."

"Judith? What are you talking about. I haven't met the girl's father—"

"No, but Suzanne has. She told him I took Beth home with me last night and he could find both of us here at the school this morning. What the hell is she playing at? Does she think it's a joke or something? We're talking about a fourteen-year-old girl who is missing, you know!"

"I do know she's missing and I hope you're not interfering again, Ms. Taylor," his voice cold as he replied.

"Again?" Judith was equally frosty. Grant softened his tone saying:

"I'm sure this Penner guy has got it wrong; Suzanne wouldn't say something like that."

"Is she there with you now? Hmm? ask her. Go ahead, I'll wait."

Judith heard Grant's exasperated sigh, but he must have covered the phone because the rest of the conversation was a mumble of noise. She could identify Suzanne's higher pitch and it sounded like they were arguing. That wasn't Judith's problem, she interrupted the quarrel loudly calling: "Hello? Hello? I'm still here."

"Sorry. It seems there has been a mix-up of some sort. Anyhow, Beth's father came back here and has filed a formal report about his daughter's disappearance so we're on top of that--"

"I made a report last night that Beth Penner was missing. Check with your dispatcher. Did Suzanne cancel that or something?"

"Well, not to say cancel but since you aren't the missing minor's legal guardian-"

"So you're telling me that the person who answered the phone at the police station yesterday only pretended to take down my report? Because I did mention I was from the school, I didn't masquerade as a parent."

"No, that report was filed but... oh hell, as I mentioned things are a bit mixed up."

Judith didn't reply and after a minute of silence Grant said:

"We've got all of our resources out pursuing this now. We will find the girl. I'm certain of it."

Oh, I am too," replied Judith, "After all you were so successful with Holly."

Chapter Twenty-Eight

Judith immediately regretted what she'd said to Grant but she'd already hung up and wasn't about to call him back. Instead, she had the ordeal of tea at the Frampton residence ahead of her.

Annalise was staying with her fiance's family for Christmas, her own parents having flown to one of their island paradise vacation homes.

It meant Judith would have to travel there alone. This felt like another thing straining her nerves and pushing her out of her comfort zone. She resented being manipulated but knew how much the school and Pat Johnson relied on the benevolence of this family.

Their annual donation covered the costs of most of the sponsored students, one of which had been Holly Lezinsky. If nothing else the family was entitled to know what had happened to its protege.

Judith realized her resentment was fuelled by the discomfort and apprehension she felt around meeting with people, especially rich people. She wished she had some of Lila's ease of manner and then thought: "Why not take Lila with me? It might be rude to bring along an uninvited guest but they're rich so I'm sure they can fix another plate."

She hurried from the office to find Lila who jumped at the chance when asked.

"Of course, I'll go with you! I'm dying to see their place; I've heard plenty about the Frampton estate. Will we really be served tea? I'd much rather try a sherry, although it's not even noon yet so I guess that's out of the question. I thought tea was a four o'clock thing?"

Judith couldn't help but laugh at the other woman's enthusiastic response. "Oh, who knows what they'll serve us. Go grab your things, we'll have to leave right away before the phones blow up again with calls and we get stuck here. I'll go warm up my car and meet you outside, it's the burgundy Subaru."

Within ten minutes they were on the road. Lila asked about the Larkin-Frampton set-up and Judith passed on what she'd learned from Pat Johnson after the principal's years of charitable association with the family.

"Audrey Larkin was widowed young due to a flying accident. Her husband was an adventurer and died flying his own plane that he kept near here at Springbank Airport. His family had money but it seems they tied it up in a trust for Noel, their only grandson.

No one knows if it was for lack of money or for companionship, but Audrey chose to move herself and Noel, who was a toddler at the time, into the home of her elder sister Eleanor. Eleanor was married to Basil Frampton. The Frampton's never had any children of their own and they helped Audrey raise Noel. This estate has been Noel's home his entire life, and he's expected to inherit everything someday.

Basil Frampton was a very wealthy man and Pat confided in me that Eleanor said he had never liked Audrey. Pat never actually met him; he'd already passed away by time Noel joined the school.

Bas, as they called him, was older than Eleanor who herself is quite a bit older than Audrey. Pat doesn't care much for Audrey either. Told me she's one of those people who let their innate racism show through even though they never say anything untoward. She said Eleanor is the exact opposite. That's the scoop on the Larkin and Frampton families."

"So, Noel has been raised as the spoiled darling in a wealthy household. He's never actually needed to get a job so it says a lot about him that he's not satisfied to live as one of the 'idle rich'. In fact, he's awfully nice considering that up-bringing."

"I agree."

Edgemont was quaintly picturesque but the enclave of estate homes on the outskirts was magnificent. They were at the opposite end of the village from the trailer park, and half the distance from the Penner household. Judith felt she was seeing the whole financial spectrum of Edgemont residences. Judith had never been to the Executive Estates subdivision before – she'd never had reason to hobnob with the wealthy!

The house was built in the English Tudor style of off-white walls and blackened cross beams and it was huge. Plenty of trees were planted throughout the property and would look lovely in the summer.

It was as pretty as a Christmas card in the winter. The windows were shuttered against the dull gray winter sky but a warm glow escaped from designs cut out of the wood. With the snow falling the whole scene was inviting and welcoming.

The two women looked at each other and Lila whistled.

"I agree, again!" said Judith.

"Seriously, though: why does Noel even bother to teach?"

"It's his vocation. His love of teaching makes him a great teacher. If he'd gone into some other kind of work the family donations would have gone to that business instead of the school so we're doubly grateful to have Noel."

They parked in the front and by the time they reached the steps a manservant had opened the double-doors and was welcoming them inside. Judith, whose coat was new two years ago but now felt distinctly shabby, was heartened by Lila's apparent lack of concern when she handed over her own duffle coat. The butler led the way to a large room where three women sat in front of the fire.

It was a beautiful room with tasteful and expensive decor and that same wealth was reflected in the occupants.

The oldest woman wore some sort of robe in gold and red brocade, her sister – the family resemblance was striking – wore a velvet dress in winter white, and Annalise was shiny in moiré silk. Judith felt that her plain shirtwaist dress and Lila's sweater and skirt looked very casual in comparison. She lifted her chin and decided she didn't care.

Annalise began the introductions but she'd never met Lila who greeted her hostesses with an apology for tagging along but said she 'couldn't resist gatecrashing to see their beautiful home'.

Eleanor Frampton was gracious, replying:

"How refreshing! We're delighted to have you, Miss Morelli."

"Oh call me Lila, please."

Audrey Larkin raised her eyebrow and looked snooty. Noel had once complained to Judith that his mother was 'awfully possessive and her behaviour towards any women of marriageable age was terrible'. Judith battled the temptation to put Mrs. Larkin's mind at ease by saying 'Neither of us are interested in your son, he's way too young in age and personality' but wisely kept silent.

"Besides", she thought, "We're obviously no threat to young Annalise who has both beauty and wealth."

They had settled into their chairs and watched as a laden tea trolley was wheeled in when a cacophony of barking erupted through the open door. A frenzied melee of snarling, snapping dogs violently entered the room and Judith was frightened as the dogs raced about fighting each other.

Lila laughed at their antics and voluntarily joined Annalise in separating the animals from what turned out to be their mode of playing to drag them out by their collars. Mrs. Larkin complained at the noise, but Mrs. Frampton was indulgent. The barking diminished as the dogs were removed further and further away from the drawing room.

Audrey Larkin started the conversation by quizzing Judith about Patricia Johnson's illness. Lila answered in her capacity as nurse to explain that the principal had a bad bout of the flu.

"I understand her secretary got it first and since the two of them are together so much it was only a matter of time before the principal got sick too."

"And you have had to step in, Bursar?"

"Judith, please, and yes I've been Principal Johnson's deputy for a number of years now. I don't have to cover for her often, but some engagements can't be scheduled outside school hours and on those occasions Pat will ask me to take her place. I will be delighted to resume my usual position when she returns."

"Do you find leadership that challenging Miss Taylor?" queried Mrs. Larkin with a sniff, refusing the familiarity of first names.

"Yes, I do when a student has been murdered and another has disappeared, and I'm supposed to be taking my annual leave."

"Who's disappeared?" asked a startled Annalise.

"Beth Penner. She didn't go home last night, and she hasn't turned up at school today. Her father's gotten the police involved. He's especially worried because Beth was best friends with Holly Lezinsky."

"Holly is the dead girl, correct?"

"Yes, that's right."

"And is it true she was murdered?" Mrs. Frampton had dropped her voice while saying the word 'murdered'.

"The police haven't come right out and said so but they are calling it an 'unlawful killing' now whereas before it was only a 'suspicious death'. I'm not sure what the distinction is but I expect it makes sense to them."

"Well, none of it makes sense to me," complained Mrs. Larkin. "I'm all confused about missing girls, and Noel said something about missing diaries, and the school play having to be cancelled for some reason. I was looking forward to seeing it on Christmas Eve day."

"They had no choice but to cancel the play, Holly had the starring role!" explained Annalise.

"Well there must have been an understudy to the lead part!"

"Audrey," intoned her sister, "think of how it would look if the play had gone ahead. These girls aren't professionals so there's none of this 'show must go on' attitude. It would be highly improper."

"And the seats would be half-empty since so many of our families are suffering from this flu bug."

"Nasty thing, the flu. You have to be very careful. We are inoculated against it every year."

"I do wish everyone was as sensible!" said Lila. "It would make my job much easier."

"The shot always makes me sick with a touch of flu for at least a day," stated Audrey Larkin.

"Oh, but you can't get the flu from the virus–" Lila started to explain but was cut off when Audrey replied:

"So, they say. But I know differently."

"Noel is the one who will be getting sick if he doesn't start taking care of himself," said Annalise with a pout. "He looks like he's hardly slept, he's lost his appetite, and have you noticed how pale he is?"

"Of course, I noticed, he is my son after all, but when I commented he snapped my head off."

"Well, he's a man, Audrey, he doesn't like to feel babied."

"A mother's concern is nothing to be ashamed of! Sometimes it's like I'm navigating a minefield, it's very tricky when you have a deeply sensitive child. Motherhood can be very trying at times."

Since none of the other women present were mothers no one responded to this.

"I hope to find out someday," said Annalise looking at Audrey Larkin. The older woman was ready to reply but her sister cut in first saying:

"Noel will make a wonderful father, and I hope he gets to have a daughter since he's so good with the girls. Now ladies, is there nothing more at all that you can tell us about this investigation?"

"There is something that isn't general knowledge yet, although I'm sure it's only a matter of time, and that is the fact that Holly was pregnant when she died." Judith's statement caused a shocked moment of silence while they mulled over this news.

"But she was just a child!" exclaimed Mrs. Frampton at the same time Mrs. Larkin burst out with:

"That's disgusting!"

"This news will knock her off the pedestal Noel has her on," put in Annalise. Again, the women were silenced while they contemplated her words.

"He's so softhearted, he'll be terribly upset when he hears about this."

"It's about time he had his eyes opened."

"I hope knowing this makes it easier for him to move on. He'll realize she wasn't the girl she made herself out to be, and that he wasn't the close confidante he thought he was."

"Holly took her troubles to Noel, did she?" asked Lila.

"All those girls do, but that Holly was the only one who ever had the nerve to phone him here at home," complained Audrey.

"Well, my dear, it will be up to you to distract him from his unhappiness, and the holidays will provide lots of opportunity." Eleanor Frampton was smiling at Annalise and didn't notice the sour look on Audrey Larkin's face.

Judith stood up and Lila hurried to her feet as well. They both felt the tension between the women and were anxious to escape. After giving fulsome thanks to their hostesses, and again admiring the beauty of the house and praising the festive Christmas decorations, they were able to leave.

Once they were in the privacy of the car Lila expelled her breath in a whoosh saying:

"Amazing visit – started with a dog fight and ended with a cat fight."

Chapter Twenty-Nine

Judith drove Lila around the Executive Estates subdivision so they could admire the Christmas decorations on the stately homes before heading back to the school. The places that were set too far back to see from the road usually had some holiday ornamentation at the end of their driveway. Lots of lanterns held by snowmen or Santas or even religious figures, and plenty of light bulbs and 'hanging icicle' lights strung along the fence.

The snow that had fallen unseasonably early this year still lay on the lawns and in the trees but the roads were in good shape for driving. Judith voiced her thought out loud:

"Considering the property taxes these homeowners must pay I guess it's only right that they get top-notch snow clearance."

"There sure are plenty of rich people living in Edgemont," said Lila, her head swivelling from one side of the road to the other.

"Especially when you add in the ranchers. They might not go for these fancy homes, but they've got money all right. Often, they look just the same as regular working-class folks with the way they dress and the vehicles they drive but many have substantial wealth, and most are very generous donors to a variety of causes."

After touring for about fifteen minutes they had their fill and Judith headed back to the school.

"When we get in can you check the answering machine for messages, especially for anything related to tonight's meeting? I want to call Dana Lezinsky."

"To invite her to the meeting?" questioned Lila, doubt evident in her voice.

"No, no. I'll tell her about it of course and if she wants me to pass on a message on her behalf I will do so. No, I need to talk to her about Billy MacNeill. Grant wants me to press charges but I want to run that idea by Dana first. If they're back together I've decided that I'll drop it."

"Oh, I do hope she doesn't take him back. He sounds a selfish type of man and any comfort he provides will be short-lived. Imagine, getting her to lie to the police when her only daughter was missing in order to protect himself!"

They separated inside the school with Judith going into Principal Johnson's office to, reluctantly, phone Dana Lezinsky. She did feel sorry about the woman's loss but knew that putting those feelings into words and listening to Dana's emotionalism would be an ordeal. She wasn't good at this sort of thing and she resented being pushed into the role. However, Pat didn't ask to get sick and Judith felt she was obligated to step up.

When the phone rang and rang she had a hopeful moment thinking she was off the hook then chided herself for being such a coward. When Dana did finally answer she sounded like she'd been sleeping.

"Dana, it's Judith Taylor from the school, I'm so sorry did I wake you?"

"No... I haven't really slept but when I sit on the couch I can doze off or zone out... something like that."

"You can't be well if you're not sleeping, are you eating? do you have any appetite?"

"I try to eat. Neighbours and friends from work – and customers even – have all been round with casseroles and easy microwave meals. I don't want to sound sorry for myself–"

"Don't worry about that, you've got a horrible tragedy to deal with and you can feel as sorry as you like. I'm afraid I'm not very good at offering comfort but if there's anything practical I can do, like phoning people on your behalf or taking you to the funeral home, anything like that you mustn't hesitate to call on me. I'm not just saying that," Judith was surprised to discover that she did mean what she said.

Dana replied: "Thank you, that helps. I'm just... I don't know, so unfocused. Nothing seems important. I just... I just miss her so much."

Judith felt at a loss and was disappointed with herself. She wanted to say the right thing but didn't know what that was. Then she realized there is no right thing to say.

"I know you do. We miss her here as well."

"Yes, she wasn't a straight-A student or anything but she had friends and she sure loved being chosen for that play. 'The play this' and 'the play that' is all we heard around here for weeks! Oh, I never thought... I guess it's cancelled."

"Yes, it has been. Well, Holly was the star."

More sobbing on the other end of the phone. Judith continued with a brisk tone of voice saying:

"Meanwhile I did call for a reason. First though, have you been seen by a doctor? you might be able to get something to help you sleep?"

"Huh! I had Billy round here offering me pills to 'take the edge off' – that's his kind of sympathy I guess – but I told him to get out and stay the hell away from me."

"Oh! So he's no longer living there with you."

"No, and good riddance. I mean look what he did, bringing the cops round when I was worried sick about Holly. What if they didn't look as hard as they should have once they knew he was in the picture?"

"Oh I'm sure that's not the case. The two police I met, well one of them is very nice and both of them are professional."

"Well, I still figure I'm better off on my own then having him here. He's a scrounger and a drunk and a waste of space!"

"You are definitely the best judge of what's right for you so 'go with your gut' as they say. And that's related to something I wanted to discuss with you. Billy showed up at the school drunk and yelling curse words, not in front of the students, they'd all gone home by then but it was... disturbing. I mentioned it to the police and they asked me to press charges. I wondered what you would think if that happened? I don't want to add to your problems."

"Go ahead! They can pile it on with his other charges. God, he's such a fool and I was too to be taken in by him. The only good thing I can say is my anger at him distracts me from this hole that Holly left behind."

Again, Judith heard sobbing and waited in uncomfortable silence. Finally, Dana gave a loud sniff and Judith said:

"I also wanted to let you know that we're having an informal parents' meeting at the school tonight and people will ask about Holly's death–"

"Her murder!"

"Yes, yes that's right. We'll share that news. We won't mention the pregnancy but if anyone does ask, we'll confirm it in case someone knows something. Someone could have seen or heard something that could lead to the father's identity and who knows what else?"

"All those parents... they're so lucky and they don't even know it! I mean I'm sure they do but not deep down where it gets you. They have no idea. I can't be around parents right now. I'm sorry but I'm not up to coming tonight." said Dana.

Judith hastened to reassure her that she wouldn't dream of asking, "I only mentioned it because I was wondering if there's anything you'd like me to say on your behalf?"

"Oh, well... people have been very kind so could you thank them for me? and tell them when they get home to give their daughters an extra-hard hug because... you just never know."

Chapter Thirty

After her meeting with the Larkin family Judith realized she's been told next-to-nothing about the investigations into Holly's death and Beth's disappearance. As Acting Head she needed to be kept up-to-date. People were expecting her to know what's going on. Especially with tonight's meeting with the parents.

"It's already been two days since Beth went missing," she reminded herself. "The police need to keep me informed."

She dialled Grant's number but once again had to leave a message. She spoke quite brusquely:

"It's Judith Taylor and I'm waiting for an update on both the Holly Lezinsky and Beth Penner cases. Please get back to me as soon as possible. Thank you."

She hadn't wanted to become involved in the investigation but the parents who phoned and came by the school, and the students, teachers, and benefactors all dragged her into it. "Forcing me into the acting administrator position has pushed my boundaries to the limit. I'm at the edge of my 'comfort zone' and itching to crawl back to the safety of anonymity so the least the police can do is help me out with this new role," she complained to herself.

"Instead, I'm stymied in every conversation. The only responses I can give are "let me find out about that" and "I'll have to get back to you" and that's the problem: I can't deal with these enquiries with a quick and easy answer. Each question always ends with me having to go chasing down an answer and then making another phone-call. It's ridiculous."

She sat there fuming over her thoughts. It was so unfair.

"And the situation with Beth is getting dire. Holly was missing for a week before her body was found, is Beth in danger, too? Does she know something that makes her a risk to someone? or is there a maniac preying on schoolgirls? What about the rest of the students? Or even the teachers – even me – if it's not some guy with a fetish about underage females. What if Beth is already dead?"

She spent a moment considering Brian Penner, Beth's father. He'd already lost his wife – how would he handle it if he lost his only child as well? Judith thought about him working two jobs to provide Beth with a good home and a good school but what did that matter if he wasn't there when she needed him? That's the sort of guilt that could – would – eat away at the survivor, especially a parent. She gave her head a quick shake to clear her thoughts. "No point imagining the worst."

At that moment her phone rang and she saw from the display that it was Grant calling. Except it wasn't, it was Suzanne using Grant's phone. She sounded amused that Judith could even imagine the police would share information with her but was quick to change her tone when Judith fought back demanding to know why Suzanne had lied to Beth's father.

"I didn't lie--," she began.

"You made up a story about me and the result was you delayed an investigation into a missing child. YOU did that, no one else, and we lost a whole night of searching because of your nonsense."

"I did nothing of the sort, I can't help if people misunderstand–"

"Why are you calling me back? I left a message for Grant, why are you using his phone?"

"I'm returning his calls while he's in a meeting with our boss, that's what partners do. At least, I thought I was returning business calls but maybe you have something else in mind?"

"What are you talking about?"

"Grant's an attractive man but don't imagine he's available because he's not."

"Well I wish he was available to answer his own damn phone," retorted Judith. "Have HIM call me when he can spare the time." And she pressed 'end call'. Slamming down the handset of a phone would have been much more satisfying. She wished now she'd called from one of the school's old-style phones.

Chapter Thirty-One

As of 5:30 pm Judith, Lila, and Marta were waiting in the lobby to welcome parents. No other teachers were attending. After ten minutes of very stilted small talk they were relieved to spot the headlights of a car turning into the school's driveway, then another, and then several cars in a cluster. It looked like they were going to get a good turnout after all.

Andrea Sealy was first through the door, "no surprise about that," thought Judith. Andrea was followed by the Rasmussens, an older couple; Brian Penner; the Grewals who brought their baby as well; another mother on her own, Debra Andrews; and a slender Chinese woman Judith didn't know. She left Lila and Marta to escort the parents to their seats while she approached the newcomer.

The woman was very chic and surprisingly tall until Judith noticed the thick platform soles on her boots. She was overdressed for a parents' meeting at the school but Judith wondered if she was going on somewhere else or had come from a formal event. Extending her hand Judith said:

"Hi, I'm Judith Taylor, School Bursar and temporary Acting Head."

The woman's small hand was cold but her smile was bright as she introduced herself saying:

"I'm Wendy Zhang, liaison for the Police Information Services."

Judith paused for a moment to consider what an unfortunate acronym that name made.

"I understand you're having a meeting with parents who are concerned and want information about the investigation into the death of your

116

student Holly Lezinsky." She pronounced Holly's surname with some difficulty, and spoke all her words with a slight accent.

"Oh I'm very pleased to meet you! We weren't too hopeful that the police would be able to send someone, and after-hours too. Thank you so much for coming."

Judith was guiding the woman towards the auditorium as she spoke. It wasn't 6:00 pm yet and she wanted to stay by the door. When they arrived in the room she waved Lila over and introduced her to Ms. Zhang.

"I'm going to wait a bit to see if anyone else is coming," she said, then in an aside to Lila added: "Watch Marta and don't let her take charge with the parents."

By time Judith got back to the entrance two more couples had arrived and another mother on her own. She ushered everyone in noticing the slushy trail across the floor despite the visitors stamping snow off their boots. Deciding "any latecomers can locate the meeting by following the wet, messy tracks," she headed into the auditorium herself.

Judith planned on standing throughout the meeting in the hopes of keeping it short but saw that Marta had placed three chairs facing the audience and she was already seated alongside Wendy Zhang.

Lila rolled her eyes at Judith when she joined them and moved to sit at the back of the room beside Brian Penner. It seemed he wanted to distance himself from the other parents and Judith sympathized, the man looked awful.

Judith welcomed the group and thanked them for coming on such short notice and at such a busy time.

"I'm very pleased to introduce you to Ms. Zhang from the Police Information Services," she said, gesturing to Wendy who immediately stood up to address the parents.

"Hello! you can call me Wendy. Thank you for giving me this opportunity to speak with you–"

Brian Penner interrupted by calling out:

"Where are the real police? Why aren't they here?"

"Why aren't they here? Well, that's because the police investigating this case are out there right now investigating."

"They better be," replied Brian but he didn't add anything further. Judith saw Lila give his hand a couple of light pats.

"Before coming here tonight to meet with you I spoke with the Senior Investigating Officer, Detective George Grant, who has given me a statement to pass on to you. He did ask that I mention to you that this information is only being given out because you are parents. He doesn't want you speaking of it to other people or the press or–"

"Does he seriously think we're going to gossip?" demanded Andrea Sealy.

"Going to gossip? no, I'm sure not, but what I'm going to tell you is sensitive to the family."

Andrea looked ready to speak again but Judith stopped her by saying:

"Please let's let Ms. Zhang, Wendy, give us the statement and then we can ask questions and have our discussion."

She sat back down with a nod to Wendy who continued:

"Thank you, Ms. Taylor. I have the statement of facts to read out." She opened a leather file folder and glanced down at the page. Speaking with care she read out the statement:

"Holly Lezinsky was aged thirteen at the time of her death. The cause of death appears to be murder, but it could possibly be an accident that was then, criminally, covered up by not notifying the authorities of the death and also by moving the body.

Her body was found by a dog-walker at approximately 11:00 in the morning. The same dog-walker, a Mrs. Kellogg, had been walking in that area several hours before and was positive the body was not there then. Mrs. Kellogg frequents that area of School Woods on a regular basis and is considered a trustworthy person and a reliable witness."

The parents were nodding at each other, complacent to be receiving these insider facts. Wendy's next comment had them exchanging shocked looks.

"At the autopsy Holly Lezinsky was found to be pregnant. The Medical Examiner advises it's too early in the pregnancy, believed to be about eleven weeks along, to determine the sex of the baby."

Brian Penner was on his feet with his fists clenched and his pale face now red.

"Holly was PREGNANT?" he bellowed.

Wendy's face was a picture of confused surprise and Judith hurried to explain to her, and any of the parents who didn't already know, that:

"Mr. Penner's daughter Beth, who is missing, was Holly's best friend."

"She can't be pregnant, she's a child. I can't believe this. Did Beth know? she must have if it's true."

"Could Beth be hiding to protect Holly's secret?" asked Debra Andrews. She was a pretty woman but her looks faded beneath a distracted air. She always acted as though her mind was somewhere else and she was worrying that she was supposed to be at some other place. It made conversation with her distracting and difficult.

"Or because she knows who the father is!" cried Brian.

The Grewals looked down at their baby peacefully sleeping in its carry cot. Mrs. Grewal straightened the blanket which was blue so Judith assumed the child was a boy then wondered if the Grewals subscribed to more modern parenting ideas.

"Did she have a boyfriend?" demanded Andrea.

Judith ignored that question. She was surprised Holly's pregnancy had even been mentioned. Turning to Wendy Zhang Judith asked if there was anything else she wanted to add.

"No there is nothing else that I want to add, but I will take questions now and hope I am able to give you some answers."

"I asked, did she have a boyfriend?" repeated Andrea.

Judith answered that question stating:

"To the best of our knowledge, no. I have spoken with Dana Lezinsky, Holly's mother, and she was quite certain about that."

"Of course, parents don't always know, do they?" Judith wondered when Marta was going to jump into the conversation. She decided to let the parents themselves argue with her over that remark, and they did.

"I know about my daughter..."

"You can't just make a blanket statement like that..."

"I know Dana Lezinsky and she's a good mother. It's wrong to imply..."

"Did Holly know she was pregnant? At that age a girl isn't necessarily regular."

Lila stood up from her seat in the back and the parents turned to her when she said:

"Holly did know, she mentioned it to me."

"Did you tell her mother?"

"I'm sorry but Holly's death doesn't release me from my legal responsibilities under the Privacy Act. Medical conversations between me and the patient and the patient's family are confidential. So I'm afraid I can't answer that. Anyhow, it isn't germane to the issue."

"Parents should be told! they have the right to know what's going on with their daughters."

Brian stood up and headed for the door adding:

"Everybody's hiding behind the red tape of can't or won't say. I've had enough of this."

He stormed out and the other parents murmured to each other. Judith believed they sympathized with the man but had been uncomfortable in his presence. She felt the same way.

Marta took the opportunity to slip out of the room as well. Judith wondered if the teacher was following Brian Penner for a private word.

Wendy Zhang also stood up to explain that it was true that the Privacy Act did tie their hands. It was something that she, as a liaison to media, dealt with every day.

"We have to be very careful protecting the rights of our citizens. The press talks about the 'right to know' but we have to do our duty, as well."

"Yes, but we're talking about minors now. As parents we truly do have the right to know what's happening with our girls. I'm sure you can understand our frustration?"

"Yes, I do understand your frustration. It's very difficult at times."

Judith listened to Wendy continually repeating phrases back and wondered if this was a technique of active listening that she'd be trained in or if she was stalling while translating in her mind. Regardless, Judith found it an annoying mannerism.

"Do you have problems with boys hanging around here at the school?" asked Mr. Rasmussen, speaking for the first time.

"I can answer that with a confident 'no,'" said Judith. "The office windows of both Principal Johnson and myself look out over the parking lot and the entrance to the school. If we ever see anyone outside one or the other of us goes and inquires about their business. It doesn't happen often but it has occurred.

In fact, back in November there was a boy who, when questioned, said he was waiting for his sister. Principal Johnson immediately called the student's mother who confirmed that yes, she'd asked her son to pick up her daughter. So we are careful. We understand that you've entrusted your children to our care and we are honour-bound to protect them."

"Of course there are males in the school itself," said Marta. Returning with a tray of Christmas goodies while Xiao followed pushing a trolley-cart loaded with cups and two large jugs of what appeared to be punch with dried bits of cinnamon and lemon peel floating in it.

Ignoring the black look Judith shot her Marta paused her statement to say: "Here's a little seasonal baking of mine. You can't visit Edgemont School at this time of year and not enjoy a nibble or a sip of something festive!"

Xiao pulled two chairs together beside the trolley and Marta set the huge tray down. The guests dutifully got up and sampled the offering. Judith and Lila abstained.

"As I was saying, we can't pretend the girls never meet men at the school because we do have male teachers." Judith kept a blank look on her face but inside she was fuming. How dare Marta start spreading malicious gossip amongst the families?

"But as you all know our teachers are vetted carefully and everyone working or volunteering in this building, male or female, has provided a Police Clearance report. Including our part-time Tae Kwan Do instructor, and the IT people at the computer lab where the older girls go for training. As I said before, we are extremely careful."

Lila chimed in to support Judith stating:

"And we are confident the police will get a result. Detective Grant has visited the school several times over the past couple of days and we've found him very helpful."

Nothing new came up in the ensuing conversation and when one couple made a move to leave the rest hurried to join them, with the exception of Andrea Sealy. She stayed behind after everyone else had said 'thank you', 'good night', and 'Happy Holidays' when they left.

Andrea wanted to speculate about Holly's pregnancy, she wanted to know where the girl had been for the week or so before her body was found, she wanted to know exactly how much Beth Penner knew and how involved she was, but of course no one could answer any of those questions. With a dissatisfied expression on her face she left, complaining that she was running late for a very important function.

Judith and Beth made no move to help Marta and Xiao clean up the mostly untouched goodies. Instead, they walked Wendy Zhang to the door thanking her for her presence.

"It made a difference and we do very much appreciate you coming to help us out."

The young woman beamed at them and they watched her until she was safely inside her car. They stayed in the foyer until Marta and Xiao appeared with their coats on. Neither carried any goodies so Judith expected the leftovers would be produced for the staff next day.

She mentally decided to bring in a couple of dozen fancy doughnuts from that new bakery near her apartment. They were sure to put Marta's treats to shame.

Chapter Thirty-Two

Judith decided that sitting in Principal Johnson's office meant she was too accessible for interruptions so she moved her laptop back to her own desk in the Library. She got herself nicely settled into the Accounts Receivable when she noticed a student wandering around the main room.

"There are only a handful of students at the school today so why can't the teachers look after them?" she grumbled, angry at herself because she forgot to put up the 'Library Closed' sign.

She decided to ignore the girl. Judith kept her head down and focused on her work but she could sense the girl moving closer. It was Margaret Sealy and she meandered over in a curious side-stepping way. Finally arriving in the doorway and hovering there, waiting to be acknowledged.

The nine-year-old daughter and only child of a neurotic and demanding mother. Judith realized she might as well get it over with saying:

"Yes, Margaret? What do you want?"

"You're not the Librarian," replied the girl."

"No, you'll have to come back later or else wait until the new year if you want to see Ms. Callahan."

"You could probably help."

"Mm, doubtful but what is it? I'll try to get you sorted and on your way. Are you looking for a particular book?"

"Actually I don't need that kind of help, I need someone to listen to my project and tell me if it's good enough or if I need to choose something else to work on over the holidays."

"Margaret, the whole point of holidays is to take a break from your chores, tasks, whatever." replied Judith.

"Don't you want to know what our project is about?"

"Not particularly," but seeing Margaret undaunted by her response she relented in order to speed things up: "Okay, tell me about it."

"Well. It's for our Natural Sciences class and we have to find an uncommon fact about an animal that is odd or something and share it with the class. The example the teacher gave us is that sharks are always swimming, even when they're sleeping, because they have to keep moving or they'll die.

So my fact is about ostriches. Now, what's the first thing you think of when you think about ostriches?"

"Hmm, I don't spend much time thinking about ostriches but let's see..." Judith was impressed by Margaret's enthusiasm and decided to play along. "When I do think of ostriches I remember that when they're scared or trying to hide they bury their heads in the sand and think nobody can see them! They're silly."

"HA!" shouted Margaret. "You're wrong! That's what everybody thinks about them, even I did before I read up on them. Ostriches don't do that."

"Oh? You mean them burying their heads in the sand is a myth?"

"No, they do bury their heads but only to protect their eggs because the nests are under the sand. It's not a scared or silly thing to do at all."

"Oh, so that's your little-known fact. I see."

"No, you don't, I haven't even told you what it is yet."

"Ah. Well please hurry along with the story."

"It's not a story. But anyhow, ostriches aren't easy to scare, in fact they're real fighters. They have two toes on each foot (most birds have three, you know) with long, sharp talons. Also, they run really fast so if an ostrich is fighting with you the only thing you can do is climb up a tree. And you have to climb high because they're also very tall and big. But they can't fly so if you can get beyond their reach, you'll be okay."

"Good to know."

"Yes, I think so too. Nobody thinks much about ostriches because they aren't pretty to look at, and because of the burying their heads in the sand thing that makes people think they're stupid or shy or cowards – but they're not. Ostriches fight back."

"Well that's a very good, unusual fact for your project, Margaret. You can go ahead and enjoy the holidays once school lets out."

"Oh I'll be here again tomorrow. My mother has an important engagement. Actually it's the Christmas get-together of her Bridge Group and she's been looking forward to it for weeks. She can't possibly cancel now. She hasn't seen any of the group for the longest time because she's been busy with her Christmas crafts and shopping and decorating. So I'll be in class tomorrow. My mother said the school is still open."

"Yes, we'll be here and it sounds like you will be as well. Why don't you go find a book with photos of ostriches and draw a nice picture of one?"

"Why don't I photocopy it?"

"Because a hand drawing takes more time which shows you've made more of an effort."

"But a photo is way more professional looking."

"True, but does a Grade Two project need to look professional?"

"I'm not in Grade Two," Margaret indignantly replied, "I'm in Grade Three!"

"Even so..."

"I've already read all of the books on ostriches but there might be something in the National Geographic magazines. I suppose I could take a look."

Without a word of thanks for the help or an apology for the interruption the girl turned away and headed to the Periodicals section.

Still," thought Judith to herself, "It is true that I never knew ostriches could fight."

Chapter Thirty-Three

Judith heard the library door open and sighed deeply. She'd put up the 'Library Closed' sign after Margaret Sealy had finally left but now someone else had entered. She sat waiting for the intruder to come and pester her. It seemed no matter where she went she couldn't escape the interruptions. She was starting to feel frustrated.

After a minute or so, when no one appeared she wondered if it was a library patron – and nothing to do with her. Lovely thought but unfortunately it didn't seem likely since she'd also turned out the lights when she'd hung up the sign. Anyone browsing for a book would switch the lights on right away. The library only had windows on one wall and the wintry December sky didn't shed much light anyhow.

Annoyed, Judith threw down her pen and marched into the main room calling:

"Who's here? what do you want?" into the darkened room but no one answered. "WHO IS THERE?" she hollered, angry now. Still, no one stepped forward.

Judith became very aware of how isolated she was in this room that anyone on the outside would think was empty. She tamped down feelings of fear because this was her realm, and she wasn't going to be chased out of it.

As she drew a deep breath to bellow her demand that the intruder reveal themself, she heard a light tap-tap and realized someone was knocking on the door. She marched over and yanked it open to see a surprised-looking Grant standing there.

"I thought that was your voice I heard," he commented. "Is everything okay?"

"No, it's not. I can't seem to get a moment's peace. I came here to get away from everyone and yet I've had non-stop visitors! Well, the last one hasn't even visited – it's somebody playing a joke, hiding out in here."

"What do you mean? There's someone else in here? In the dark? Well let's put on the lights--" but he didn't get the chance to complete his sentence before a figure came hurtling from behind the stacks and knocked Grant to the ground before fleeing out the open door.

Judith was startled and bent to help Grant up, she never even thought of pursuing the person. Grant struggled to his feet and hurried into the hall but there was no sign of anyone in either direction.

"Who was that?" he demanded.

"I have no idea. I heard someone come in but when I called out to them they didn't answer. I thought it must be one of the girls playing games."

"That was no girl, that was a man. What did he want in here? with you?"

The stared at each other for a moment and Judith felt fearful. Grant's look was full of concern yet she hadn't even considered that she might have been in any kind of danger. But why would a man skulk around in the dark library, drawing her out of her room with his silence? Was he waiting to catch her unawares? waiting to pounce?

"Was it that Billy MacNeill again?"

"No, definitely not. He's in jail."

"You've caught him! Where's Beth?"

"No, sorry, we arrested Billy MacNeill on other charges. He has an alibi for when Holly went missing and for the time when her body got dumped outside your woods.

He did want an alibi from Dana Lezinsky but only to prevent us discovering his other crime. He's involved in what's called a 'chop shop': stolen cars dismantled – chopped up – for parts that are sold out of the country. The garage is in Calgary, and he was there for several days over the time period in question."

"So he didn't kill Holly and he doesn't have Beth."

"We don't know that anyone actually has Beth. She might be hiding for reasons of her own."

"For this long? No, I can't believe that. Beth is a quiet girl – Holly was the leader in that friendship, she had all the initiative. I can't see Beth staying away on purpose. She'd have to realize her father is worried sick."

"But maybe worrying him – punishing him – is the point? I seem to remember that the girls I knew as a teenager all hated their parents."

"Hmm, Beth does have a lot of autonomy for a girl her age and it could be that she's a bit resentful and is trying to get her father's attention. I suppose that's possible, it's not something I would have imagined though."

"You've always had a good relationship with your father, then?"

"Oh no. Well yes, Dad was great, but he died when I was quite young so I really can't say."

"I'm sorry to hear that. It must have been hard growing up without him."

"Yes actually, it was..." Judith paused for a moment remembering and Grant gave her space. "But getting back to the intruder – if it wasn't Billy MacNeill, and it wasn't a student, who could it be?"

"Judith, I mean Ms. Taylor--"

"Judith is fine."

"Thank you. Judith, is anyone angry with you for some reason?"

"Other than Suzanne Mireau?"

"I'm being serious. Could anyone have any reason to harm you?"

"No! Why would they?"

"Could they think you know something that could shed light on Holly's murder?"

"It is murder for sure, is it?"

"Yes, I'm afraid so. Well, moving the body made murder seem probable although someone could do that trying to cover up a drug overdose or something. However, the coroner has now confirmed that evidence of perimortem bruising and injury has shown that the blow to the head wasn't accidentally inflicted."

"Poor girl."

"Especially since she didn't die immediately. There's no way to know for sure but it's possible that if whoever hit her had called 9-1-1 something could have been done to save her."

"So, the poor girl lay there dying alone until that person came and moved her."

"We don't know that she was alone, and it was only a matter of an hour or two – not days."

"But she was either killed and her body stored somewhere, or kept alive for days and then killed. Either scenario is awful to contemplate. All the while we were thinking she'd run off with some boy she was dead or being held prisoner. So what about Beth? We can't be sure she's playing up to get back at her father, what if she's been imprisoned too?"

"Could someone think Beth has been in touch with you? Could that be the reason this person broke in?"

"But I wasn't able to get hold of Beth! I went to her house, I've phoned repeatedly, her father came to the school to talk to me. By the way I let your Suzanne know what I thought about her for that."

"She's not 'my' Suzanne. So, you called her to talk?"

"We talked but I didn't call her I called you. Look, I've been pretty frustrated with everyone asking me questions and me not knowing anything despite having to be in charge here at school so I phoned you to get some answers. I left a message. Since you were in a meeting with your boss Suzanne returned the call."

"Wait a sec, I want to be absolutely clear about this: Suzanne answered a message you'd left for me on my phone?"

"Yes, but I didn't mind. It was a business call after all, no matter what she said."

"What did she say?"

"I forget the exact words – something about you not being available. As if I care whether or not you're married or her boyfriend or anything."

"I'm not married, and I don't have a girlfriend. And I would never choose Suzanne to be my girlfriend."

"Grant you don't need to explain your personal life to me. It's none of my business," said Judith, feeling a little puzzled by the look Grant was giving her.

She felt her head spin with thoughts of the intruder, of Beth, of Holly, and Billy MacNeill having an alibi. Unaccustomed tears threatened to spill and she turned away from Grant and headed back into her office. He followed but she told him her head was pounding and all she wanted was to be alone.

"I'm sorry Judith but I don't think you should be. At least, not here in the library. Go to the staff-room or get someone to stay in the principal's office with you. We can't be sure that the man who sneaked in here isn't hiding somewhere else in the building."

"Oh great, that's helped my headache enormously. Thank you so much."

"I'm sorry, but I want to keep you safe."

"No Grant, I'm the one who should apologize. I realize you're a policeman who is only doing his job. If it wasn't so early in the day I would go home."

Grant's manner was diffident as he asked, "Would there be anyone at home to keep you company?"

"No, I live alone but I have been thinking of getting a cat."

Chapter Thirty-Four

Judith walked through the school hallways opening each classroom door and checking to see if there was a teacher or any students inside. Grant trailed along behind, keeping her company until she paired up with someone else. Safety in numbers. Judith still believed the incident in the library must have been a prank of some sort, she couldn't think of any reason why anyone would want to harm her.

"Oh and I'm sorry but I forgot – I should have thanked you for sending Ms. Wendy Zhang along to our Parents' Meeting. She was very nice and, surprisingly considering our parents, we only had one brief issue when she caused offence by warning them off talking to the press. You know," she stopped and gave him a searching look,

"It really is something that the media hasn't been camped out on our front lawn. I mean the murder of a young student, who was pregnant, at an All-Girls School – those are all the ingredients for over-the-top sensationalism and lurid headlines. Honestly, it's a wonder they've left us alone."

"I suspect you can thank Eleanor Frampton for that. She's got 'friends in high places' and with her nephew working here well... money talks."

"Well, I can only say that I hope it keeps talking until we shut down for the year."

"It is a nice break not to have my footsteps dogged by shouting reporters pushing their microphones and cameras in my face. It's so difficult to shake the press once a story hits the headlines."

"Oh of course, the party! That will explain it."

They'd resumed walking but this time it was Grant who stopped and turned to Judith saying that didn't explain anything to him.

"There's a big party scheduled for the 24th to celebrate Noel Larkin's birthday and Christmas. It's an annual event and sounds like quite the gala. All kinds of bigwigs and assorted influential people will be attending and they certainly won't want to fight their way through a crowd of reporters going in and coming out again. It's probably some high-profile invitee who has brought pressure on the media."

"I didn't know anything about this party, I wasn't invited," said Grant.

"No? I'm not going either," Judith replied, ending that conversation.

Continuing down the corridor she discovered two teachers with only a handful of students in two classrooms and suggested they might like to join up in one room and have a singsong or play a game. The teachers were happy to comply.

With renewed determination Judith headed for the staff room. She stifled a giggle at the image of herself elbowing open the bat-wing doors of the saloon in an old-fashioned Western looking for a showdown but that's how it felt.

Over these past few days Judith had come to realize how much animosity there was between the teaching and the administrative staff. She felt it was one-sided, on the teachers' part, but was honest enough to admit that she'd never made any friendly overtures herself.

Perhaps Lila, with her fun and friendly attitude, would be the one to bridge the gap.

Grant left her outside the staff room door saying he'd check in again later. When Judith stepped out of the alcove silence descended on the room but she didn't get the impression they'd been talking about her. Which made a nice change.

"Where's Cindy Callahan?" she asked.

"The Librarian went home because there are no Library Classes today," said Xiao in a sulky, challenging manner. Marta was quick to jump in and add:

"And Cindy wasn't feeling too well. She worried that she might be coming down with the flu bug and didn't want to pass it around."

Xiao caught on and hurried to add,

"Yes, that's right. Cindy said she was ill so it was lucky she didn't have Library Classes."

"I hope she doesn't have the flu, that would ruin her holidays," replied Judith mildly. Marta and Xiao looked at her warily but the other teachers in the room regarded her with interest.

"A student came into the library while I was in my office and I don't want the girls wandering around the school unsupervised."

"Well, you can't expect us to babysit!" exclaimed Xiao.

"If that's what you call looking after your young charges then yes, that's exactly what I expect."

"We don't work for you." Marta chimed in.

"No, but you do work for the parents of the girls who are in this school today. I saw that Jennifer and Joanna each only had a few students so they've combined into one classroom. What I want to know is does anyone have any ideas about entertaining the students along with keeping an eye on them?"

Tanya, who taught History and Science, spoke up:

"What about watching a movie? Eddie, I've got the DVDs I borrowed from you in my bag because I wanted to return them before the holidays. It's 'The Bill Murray Collection' and it includes the movie 'Scrooged.'"

"There's a DVD player in the Library," said Judith. "That sounds like a very good idea that should see us through pretty much to the end of the day. In fact, we could do this again tomorrow if any students show up."

"Is 'Scrooged' age-appropriate?" asked Marta.

"Let's see what it says on the box," answered Tanya. She went to her locker and took out a bag with a set of DVDs inside and read the cover.

"It says PG-13 but I watched the movie a couple of nights ago and honestly there's nothing to worry about for the younger students. Just like with Bugs Bunny cartoons – the adult allusions will go over their heads."

"I've got other Christmas movies I can bring in for tomorrow," said Eddie. "I've got 'Elf' and 'The Santa Claus' and, well I guess 'Bad Santa' isn't a good idea..." The teachers who knew that movie laughed along with him.

"That's great, thanks, all of you, for helping out. I'll go see if I can find some snacks in the kitchen."

"I'll get this movie set up," said Eddie with Tanya adding that she'd round up the kids and bring everyone to the Library.

"I guess I'll stay here and listen for important phone messages – like from the police or even another one from Beth Penner." Marta's comment had a chilling effect but Judith chose to let it pass and simply said:

"Thank you, Marta. That will be a great help."

Tanya and Eddie left the staff-room with her. In the corridor Tanya stopped Judith saying:

"We've been discussing something and want you to know that there's been some talk, and I know it's second-hand gossip but anyways, some of the students have told teachers that they saw Noel Larkin kissing Holly Lezinsky."

"What! Noel? No, that.. well, what do you think? Are they making it up?"

"No," said Eddie explaining: "It not only the students who have seen things. I've witnessed stuff myself but what I saw seemed innocent. I don't want to imply that there's been any kind of wrongdoing, but I do think you should know that things are being said."

"To give you a heads-up, like," added Tanya.

"I appreciate that. Stepping into the principal's shoes, even just for a few days, is burden enough without being blindsided if I'm questioned by a parent about this. So, what exactly have you heard, and seen?"

The two teachers signalled to each other with their eyes and then spoke quickly as though relieved to get it out.

"This usually just happens at rehearsals, but they do stuff like hold hands and exchange notes and laugh together over private jokes."

"They whisper and giggle a lot."

"The other girls in the play became quite jealous of all the attention Noel was giving to Holly but that could be explained by the role she was playing. They've written their own play so I don't know details but

Holly was the lead and Noel said it was all part of the coaching. That could be true."

"Has anything like this happened with other students, in leading roles in the plays from other years?"

"I never heard any rumours until Holly got cast as the star."

"Ah, it sounds like you think it might be what, sour grapes or something?"

"Or it could be because Holly is now a tragic-romantic figure, at least to adolescent girls. Kind of a Juliet Capulet."

"Yes, I see. Do you think I should say anything to the police about the tales?" Judith was actually wondering if the two teachers were telling her this hoping for that exact result but instead they said:

"Oh, I don't know if I'd go that far."

"It could cause problems – unfairly, like."

"You're right. They don't know Noel like we do and anything like this well, I wouldn't want to give them ideas. The lead detective seems very level-headed, but his partner is definitely given to flights of fancy. It's enough that we know about the rumours and can quash any speculation or exaggerations."

"That's right. We felt you should know, but a teacher's reputation is easy to tarnish with innuendo."

"Especially a male teacher in an all-girls school!"

"Thank you very much for passing this on." After they separated Judith found herself speculating about Noel and Holly. She couldn't believe he could be so foolish but if Annalise was anything like Cindy Callahan then all of her conversation would revolve around the wedding with questions like what colour for this? who should sit where? what kind of music? Holly, on the other hand, could provide Noel with the true 'girlfriend experience'. Starry-eyed admiration, a young girl's innocent delight, sweet stolen kisses... enough to turn any man's head.

She was glad the teachers hadn't urged her to pass their information on to the police.

Chapter Thirty-Five

A search of the kitchen cupboards unearthed an unopened box of microwave popcorn. Judith zapped several bags which made a horrible stink but were welcomed with enthusiasm by the moviegoers.

She saw them all settled then went into her office to finish her Accounts Receivable work. She wanted to come back after the holidays to a fresh start.

She thought it likely that most people felt this way in January. Of course, academics and other school workers also felt this in September. Judith started at Edgemont School for Girls almost ten years ago so her life followed the rhythm of the school year although she didn't get to stop work for ten weeks each summer.

While at University she'd applied for entry-level positions at several accounting firms who offered placements to graduates. She'd been accepted by a few of them since her grades were very good. She chose the largest company but found it to be a soulless environment. Sitting in a cubicle working her way through that day's assignments wasn't particularly fulfilling but that wasn't the problem. It was overhearing a comment her boss made to his boss that disillusioned Judith.

The man was boasting that he only hired what he called 'the perfect accounting personality type' and went on to disparage all of his employees for being timid and easy to burden with extra work. Some of them could be attractive – if they'd made an effort – but with no social graces. Easy to intimidate, subordinate, fearful little people. Judith had burned with shame hearing his contemptuous words spoken so condescendingly.

That's when she resolved to find a job where she could be in charge of her own domain and Edgemont School was the answer. She was over-qualified for the work, and it meant a drop in pay, but Judith settled well into the school environment. It was Principal Johnson who hired her and Judith was grateful that the woman was willing to take a chance on her. Both of them were satisfied with the result.

She looked out of her office window to her view of the parking lot and a bit of the front driveway. The sky was full of snow and a sleety mix was falling. Not a pleasant day.

Judith thought about the scheduled vacation she'd been forced to forego and decided she wasn't missing out on anything. Her plan had been to drive to various hiking trails in Kananaskis Country and enjoy bracing fresh air and the quietude of a snowy mountain landscape. Winter in southern Alberta meant cold temperatures with sunny skies of bright blue but so far this year the weather was milder and wetter.

Even if the weather had co-operated the shortened days would have meant long nights indoors on her own. She had books to read, streaming TV to watch, and an Internet connection but the restlessness she'd been feeling the last few days made her dissatisfied with her own company.

It was odd, she'd never acknowledged being lonely before, but she suspected that's what she was feeling now. The thought of a cute kitty was even more appealing.

She shut down her laptop and turned out the office light before joining the others to watch the rest of the movie.

Chapter Thirty-Six

After the movie was over Judith was tidying up the library when Lila walked in saying:

"Aha! so this is where you've been. I thought the handsome detective might have whisked you away for a tete-a-tete."

"Don't be silly." Judith was embarrassed to feel her cheeks get warm. "Where have you been?"

"Tending to the sick. We've got one teacher and a couple more students down with the flu. I've been nursing them until someone could come pick them up. The flu is an awful illness and people don't give it the respect it deserves. I can't understand why people don't get the flu vaccination: it's free and it's easy to get. I hope you take the shot."

"Every year. I had flu once and let me tell you, when you're single and you've got the flu it's the worst. I was only bad for about three days but those three days were utterly miserable. I piled every blanket I owned – plus my winter coats – on top of me and I was still shivering. In fact, I thought I had bugs crawling on me and when there was nothing to see I was afraid I was hallucinating. Turned out that sweat was pouring out of my skin so fast it felt like insects running up and down my sides!

I lay there sweating and shivering and wishing someone would run me a bath and then wash my sheets while I was in it but of course there was no one to do that so I suffered and felt sorry for myself. I've gotten the flu shot every year since!"

"The flu is a killer, especially of the elderly, and people end up in hospital because of dehydration. It's a shame you had to learn the hard way but at least you did learn something. What about other vaccines?"

"I've had the one for shingles and when I reach age 65 I'll get the pneumonia shot as well. Our benefit plan paid for most of my shingles vaccine and the pneumonia one is free for seniors."

"Hmm, might not be by time you're a senior."

"Oh great, thanks for that..."

"I only meant it's because you're too young to be talking about what you'll be doing as a senior."

"I know how old you are, Lila, and I'm the same age. Anyhow, if I have to buy that shot I will do so."

"Yeah, it was the shingles vaccine I was wondering about and I'm glad to hear you got it. That is a nasty infection and it's extremely painful, too."

"I heard that if you get shingles around your waist and the circle of rash joins up you'll die but that's just an old wives' tale, right?"

"Right, but you'd be in such agony you might wish you were dead!"

"I knew someone who had it when she was younger than me and she recommended I get the vaccine so I did."

"Good for you. That's being sensible. Now, let's move away from sensible and into the realm of speculation..."

"What do you mean?"

"Welllll, let's be BFFs and you tell me your deepest, darkest secrets. What's been on your mind lately?"

"As a matter of fact, I've been thinking about buying a mobile home."

"What?"

"Yeah, I rent right now, and it will take forever for me to afford to buy but when I visited Dana Lezinsky at the Trailer Park I was impressed. It wasn't at all like what I thought it would be. The whole complex is very well-kept and the actual trailers are quite roomy and—"

"Stop! that's not what I'm talking about! I want to hear what's happening with you and Grant."

"Me and Grant? Nothing. There's nothing happening, why would there be?"

"Well he likes you and don't you think he's good-looking? His colouring is unusual and he's very attractive."

"Mmm, yeah. I suppose he is."

"You suppose?"

"I've never been attracted to blond men. Except for Peter O'Toole in 'Lawrence of Arabia', that is."

"Oh God yeah, when the camera does that close-up of his blue eyes in his sunburnt face... to die for!"

"True! but Grant doesn't have that colour of hair or eyes: he's white-blond with pale blue compared to Peter O'Toole's yellow-blond with bright blue."

"But he's got a look that's so, I don't know, aloof or something? Totally hot, eh?"

"That reminds me – if we're going to tell-all what's the scoop about you being married? Where's your husband?"

"Oh, that's a story for another day. I'll require a whole bottle of wine all to myself before I can get into that tale. Hey, I would actually be drinking the whole bottle since you are my non-drinking companion. But anyways I asked first. So, tell me the truth: you aren't interested in Grant?"

"As anything other than the detective who I hope is going to solve this case? no, I'm not. I'm not looking to meet anyone. Do you remember that old Simon and Garfunkle song 'I Am A Rock?' well, that's me. I'm a rock that feels no pain."

"Nobody can love a rock, Judith."

"Love? I will fall in love when... hmm, I can't say when hell freezes over because climate change, eh?"

"Omigod you made a joke! Now stop avoiding the question and tell me what you think of Grant?"

"Okay, he's personable and yes, he is good-looking, seems intelligent and common sensical and I expect he'd make a great friend but that's it, that's all I feel."

"Really?"

Judith laughed saying: "You sound disappointed."

"I am! First of all because he's I can see that he's interested in you, and secondly it would put that Suzanne in her place, and thirdly I'm a born matchmaker. So if not Grant what about Brian Penner?"

"Brian Penner! are you serious? the man's told us repeatedly that he's frantic over his daughter. Finding Beth is the only thing on his mind, why would you even think about him in those terms?"

"Because he's drop-dead gorgeous, that's why!"

"He's… yeah, I guess but sorry, I can't get past his red-rimmed eyes from tears or lack of sleep or both."

"Well I didn't put your phone number in his phone for nothing you know."

"Lila!"

"Oh don't Lila me, he's extremely handsome and so macho too."

"I don't believe you," said Judith, shaking her head. She wasn't sure how serious Lila was being, this kind of bantering back and forth was a new experience for her.

"And I don't think I believe you about Grant being only a friend. You told me that you've called him a couple of times…"

"As part of his job, and my job. That's it."

"Mmm, so you say.."

"It's true. Grant is nothing more than like a work colleague and even that's only going to be temporary. Until the cases are solved."

"'Methinks the lady doth protest too much.'"

"I'm not! Believe me the last thing I'm looking for is a date. And by the way I'm not Lady MacBeth."

"Oh, is that where that's from? I thought it was Hamlet."

"You're right it is."

"Good way to change the subject, Judith. Anyhow I heard some of the girls singing in the hallway *Cop and Bursar sitting in a tree, k-i-s-s-i-n-g, first comes love'–*"

"No students were singing that! although I wouldn't put it past the teachers!"

"They left the library laughing and there was Grant waiting in the hall.

"What are you doing here again?" asked Judith.

"I wanted to discuss something with you. About the case."

Lila smiled and gave them a little wave as she walked on. They could hear her singing softly:

"...'then comes marriage, then comes baby in a baby carriage.'"

Grant raised an eyebrow at Judith who felt her cheeks blush as she hurried to explain:

"That was something from the movie we watched. Anyhow, you said you had something to discuss?"

"I'd rather not have the conversation here, if you don't mind, could we go get a Tim Horton's or something?"

"Oh, sure. Before we go let me check for messages on the answering machine and I'll grab my coat and meet you out front."

"I'll walk with you, and you can tell me more about this movie you saw."

Judith gave him a sharp glance, but his expression was bland.

Chapter Thirty-Seven

None of the messages on the school's answering machine required a call back so Judith grabbed her coat and she and Grant headed out of the building. Unfortunately, they were forced to stay by the presence of Margaret Sealy in the foyer.

"Why are you still here, Margaret?"

"No one came to pick me up."

"Alright, who can we call to come and get you?"

"There's only my mother and I've called and called. There's no answer. I left a message on the home phone, and I even called her cellphone – although I'm not supposed to – and left a message there. Why do people carry phones around with them if they're not going to answer them?"

"It looks like something's come up. Whereabouts do you live?"

"At the Executive Estate."

"Oh, that's where Mr. Larkin lives, right?"

"Yeah, his home is a couple of houses down. Sometimes Mr. Larkin takes me home but I haven't seen him today."

"No, I haven't seen Noel either. He should have been in school today. If he called in someone else took the message. Well, that's okay I will drive you home. Phone back your mother at both numbers and leave a message to let her know."

She turned to Grant saying:

"We'll have to have that discussion another time. I'll be here again tomorrow."

"Actually, it would be much better to do it tonight. You'll understand when I explain everything. Look, why don't I come with you two and after we drop off Margaret," he looked at the girl and smiled a hello, "we can grab a coffee then. Or we can talk in the car on the return trip."

"I can't get into a car with a stranger," announced Margaret.

"But I'm not a stranger and it's my car so that should be okay."

"I don't think so. He's still a stranger."

"He's a policeman."

"Are you? Can I hold your gun? Do you have a badge?"

"Yes. No. Yes, again – would you like to see it?"

Margaret giggled at his answer and Judith was surprised because Margaret was definitely not a giggly type of girl. She decided Grant's looks must be more appealing than she thought.

"Yes, I need to know what it says. What's your name? and don't look at the badge before you tell me."

"My name is George Grant and I'm a detective." He handed over the slim wallet that housed his badge and Margaret inspected it carefully – even running her finger over the embossed lettering.

"Okay Detective George Grant, you can accompany us in Ms. Taylor's car," she decided.

Judith locked the front door and they hurried to the car park. The air was cold with a chilly dampness but at least the drizzle of sleet had stopped. The parking lot was slippery underfoot but once they got on the main road the salt and gravel laid down by the maintenance crews had done its job and the tires got traction.

Margaret chattered away. She discussed the plot of "Scrooged" and explained which parts of the movie she loved and which she hated. Margaret Sealy didn't like or dislike, she lived her emotions to the extreme.

"It sure wasn't like the real movie."

"It was a real movie, Margaret."

"You know what I mean. The one where Alistair Sims plays Scrooge, and he wears a funny nightgown and a hat with a tassel. That was way better."

"The actor's name is Sim, not Sims. But I agree with you, I preferred the original."

"I don't think that is the original, there was one made in the thirties," commented Grant.

"Really? who was in that version?"

"Oh, I've no idea, I never saw it. In fact I haven't seen 'Scrooged', I've only seen the Alistair Sim one. I liked it."

"I loved it," replied Margaret. "But you know, the character of Scrooge might only pretend to change because he got scared by the ghosts. After awhile he might not change at all."

"Hmm, that's quite insightful for someone in Grade Three, Margaret. What do you think, Grant?"

"Yes, but there's another layer of truth that you haven't reached yet."

"What do you mean?"

"Well, there's the top layer – the surface – where Scrooge has his eyes and his purse opened. And then there's the second layer – his subconscious – where he's been frightened by the ghosts and thoughts of his own mortality into behaving properly. Are you with me so far?"

"Yes, of course, what's the next layer?"

"Ah, that's his heart and soul. In his heart of hearts, he always knew his greed was wrong. Greed is one of the Seven Deadly Sins, but he conveniently forgot that. But the soul wants to be good and to do the right thing so when the opportunity arose his heart and soul conquered his miserliness, chased away his fears, and opened him up to love."

Nine-year-old Margaret Sealy only understood half of what Grant said but from the look on her face and in her shining eyes he'd won her over completely. She loved him with the sudden devotion of an awestruck child. Judith found herself feeling a bit sentimental as well.

Then Margaret broke the spell by saying: "So it's like the World Wide Web, the Deep Web, and the Dark Web, right?"

"What on earth do you mean? What are all these 'webs', Margaret?"

"Oh, you know, Ms. Taylor. The World Wide Web is what everybody goes on when they're surfing the Internet. The Deep Web is where the banks and you know, hospitals, put their secret stuff. Everybody can go into the Deep Web but only if they have the right log-in passwords. Then there's the Dark Web where all the criminals hang out and do crime. I don't know much about it because every computer I get to use has parental controls on it. Even the floor models at Best Buy!"

Judith looked helplessly at Grant who turned to look at Margaret who hung over the back of his seat.

"Are you wearing your seat-belt?"

"Is that all you've got to say?"

"I know you heard me, but I'll repeat myself: are you wearing your seat-belt?"

Margaret flung herself back and they heard a click as she buckled up.

"There are you happy now?"

"Ecstatic."

"So, are the Scrooge layers like the web layers? You didn't answer."

"I'm afraid to answer a child as precocious as you."

Margaret thought that reply was hilarious. Looking out the car window she hollered:

"You passed it. Back up, back up!"

Judith complied and pulled into the driveway of a house with an ultra-modern design. The facing wall was blank but huge slanted windows ran up both sides. Andrea Sealy stood in the entrance holding the door open. She was wearing her coat, hat, and boots evidently having just arrived home herself. Margaret hopped out of the car saying:

"Thank you for the ride, Ms. Taylor. Bye," and ran halfway up the brick walkway before spinning round to yell:

"Goodbye to you too, Detective George Grant."

As Judith reversed out of the driveway back onto the road Grant commented:

"Are they all like that?"

Chapter Thirty-Eight

Judith continued driving away from the village centre towards the highway. That's where the Tim Horton's and other fast-food franchises were located.

As Grant made easy conversation, she realized that he was the first man to ever sit in her car. Judith was aware of the intimacy of the two of them travelling in a darkened car but felt completely comfortable. She was starting to see Grant as the man who could possibly be a friend instead of just Grant the policeman.

When they arrived at the coffee shop and saw the harsh indoor lighting Judith suggested they use the drive-thru and have their coffee and discussion in the parking lot. Grant readily agreed saying:

"You're not going to like what I have to say so it's best to have the conversation in private."

"That sounds ominous. Although if you're willing to be out in public having coffee with me, I guess I'm not on the verge of arrest!"

"Not you, but... let's get settled first."

They were served with coffees – his a double-double, hers milk only – and doughnuts – his a Boston Cream, hers a plain old-fashioned – with quick efficiency and were soon parked in a far corner of the lot. Each half-turned in their seat to face the other and use the cup holders for their hot drinks.

"What I'm about to tell you is in confidence. The decision stems from a meeting I had yesterday with my boss. I don't agree with the action we're about to take but I gave my opinion and that's that. I have to do what I'm told which is bring in Annalise Sutherland for questioning in the death of Holly Lezinsky."

"WHAT? Annalise? No way."

"Well, there's evidence of trouble between her and Holly. We have witnesses to an argument Annalise had with Noel about Holly, also another person witnessed Annalise having a very heated discussion with Holly herself."

"How did you find these witnesses? There were no interviews with students in the school because I would have had to be present if that was the case."

"You're right, I would have called on you to be the 'appropriate adult' but these witnesses, and yes, they were students, came to us at the police station."

"But they're teenagers!"

"They came with an adult, that teacher I met at the school, Marta Smith."

"Oh, Good Lord. She's such an interfering, nasty... ugh! Please tell me what happened, what was said, and when."

"They came in yesterday. Remember she was out front along with Suzanne and me when you arrived?"

"Yes, I was a bit late. Despite driving slowly, I was still clipped in a fender bender."

"Why didn't I know about that?"

"Because I never had a chance to say anything before Suzanne attacked me about playing Nancy Drew, remember?"

"Right. Well, your car seems to be running fine, is your bumper damaged?"

"I have no idea, I forgot to look. If there's anything it won't be much and, after all, that's what bumpers are for."

"You didn't look? What about the other car, did you look at that?"

"Oh, sorry I didn't explain. The other car didn't even stop. He, or she, was driving right behind me – and following too close – the whole way to school but when I arrived all of a sudden the car sped past me dinging my rear bumper in the process."

"A hit-and-run. Doesn't sound like you got a licence plate, or did you?"

"No, I was too busy trying to control my car from skidding straight into one of those big old trees that line the road just there. I was lucky that I didn't hit anything and was able to get into the driveway."

"I'm sorry to hear about this and sorry too that you never got a chance to mention it. You must have been pretty shaken up."

"I was, but the argument with Suzanne did a great job of putting it out of my mind!" she said with a laugh. "Anyhow, go on with what you were saying about Marta."

"Oh yes. Well, while we were waiting for you Marta said she had someone who wanted to talk to me about Holly's case but not at the school so could she bring them to the police station? I said 'of course' and we arranged a time.

When she arrived, she actually had three teenagers with her. Two of them didn't do much more than nod but the third girl made a clear statement and answered all the questions we put to her.

She's stated that Annalise often dropped by during rehearsals and on one occasion, shortly before Holly disappeared, when Annalise arrived she caught Noel with his arm around Holly's shoulders. The two of them were reading her part in the script but Annalise started yelling that she was 'fed up with his behaviour with this girl'. Everyone at the rehearsal heard it and Noel grabbed Annalise by the arm and drew her away from the stage where everyone was watching. It seems Annalise didn't lower her voice and didn't care who heard her.

They couldn't hear Noel's side of the conversation because he kept his voice low, but it was obvious he was trying to calm her down. The girl—"

Judith interrupted asking: "Which girl?" but Noel shook his head and said they were minors, and he wasn't naming any names. Then he continued with the statement:

"So, the girl reported that Annalise said things like 'he needed to get his head straight' and 'why was he jeopardizing everything?' and 'why this girl? what's so special about her?'. I gather the whole cast was eagerly listening to every word. Afterwards they talked about nothing else and when Holly went missing, they discussed telling someone and finally chose Ms. Smith as their confidante. 'Because she heard us talking about it anyhow and asked for an explanation' the girl told me.

I asked Ms. Smith why she hadn't passed the information on to the police, but it seems she thought the girls had 'blown the whole thing out of proportion in order to dramatize themselves'. Once Holly's body was discovered the girls were afraid to say anything because they didn't want to get Mr. Larkin in trouble. None of them seem to care too much for or about Annalise Sutherland."

"No, I expect they're jealous of her engagement to Noel."

"Sounds to me like there's plenty of jealousy going around."

"Ha! you haven't met Mrs. Larkin, Noel's mother, yet. She's the most possessive of them all! But you can't seriously think Annalise kidnapped this girl, killed her, held her body for days – God knows where because she's staying at Noel's place for the holidays – then put her in a car and dumped her in the woods. I don't even know if Annalise can drive, she's always got a chauffeur when she comes to the school."

"I pointed out the unlikelihood of Ms. Sutherland being able to do any of those things and my superior said it was up to me to figure out how it was done because, obviously, it was done."

"That's helpful. So tonight you're going to go to the Larkin's home to arrest Annalise?"

"Not arrest and not tonight. No, I'll be picking her up tomorrow morning and taking her into the police station for questioning. I'm sure they'll call a lawyer for her and we're hoping we'll get a statement. I have to act on the evidence and if the Sutherlands and Larkins weren't such influential people I bet I would have been given a warrant for her arrest but for now I only get to ask questions."

"That's all to the good actually because I'm sure she didn't do it and this way you won't get sued for wrongful arrest."

"If she's got an alibi the whole thing won't take long at all."

"But an alibi for when, exactly?"

"Exact is the one thing we can't be. However, we know Holly left the school about 17:30 on December 12th but she never arrived home. She was by herself having told Beth Penner that she didn't want company, she 'had some thinking to do' on her own."

"Wait a minute, that reminds me: is there any news about Beth?"

"No, nothing yet. We've talked to classmates and neighbours, took her photo round the malls and the video arcade at the movie theatre but no luck so far. We believe she's hiding out with a friend who is keeping it quiet at Beth's request."

"Oh. That's disappointing of Beth. Anyhow, sorry to interrupt – go on."

"So, the time period needing to be alibied is the evening and night of December 12th for sure. Then, in general, what the person was doing over the next few days, and finally a witness to their activities early on the morning of the 19th, since Holly's body was discovered mid-morning and she hadn't been lying there all night."

"What about this other accusation about Annalise and Holly quarrelling?"

"That came from Marta Smith herself. She says she saw Holly go chasing down the hallway after Annalise and then, when she caught up with her, having an intense conversation that turned into a real argument and ended with Annalise shoving Holly away and marching off. We don't know if it was the same day as the Annalise and Noel argument, but it doesn't seem likely. I can't see Noel letting Annalise leave by herself, not when she was so upset with him."

"I see that you need to speak to Annalise based on all this but I'm certain, absolutely certain, that there's no way she killed Holly."

"I agree with you but it's the facts that need to be in agreement. I'll know more tomorrow after the interview."

"Will you let me know?"

"I'll call you for sure." Judith felt Grant's gaze intensify. She caught her breath and let her eyes stare into his. It felt like a long moment before she was forced to exhale. Without a word she started the car and drove them back to the school.

Chapter Thirty-Nine

Normally the Senior Investigating Officer and his partner wouldn't pick up a suspect to bring in for questioning, that was a job for patrolmen. But since Annalise Sutherland came from such a high-profile family, and since she was currently staying with her fiancé at the Larkin-Frampton residence, another powerhouse family, Grant and Suzanne were in attendance.

Judith heard both Grant's and Noel's version of the incident.

All members of the household gathered in the front hall while Annalise was asked to accompany the two detectives to the police station for further questioning, and to make a statement. This action was met with outrage, disbelief, tears, and temper.

"Noel, do something!" cried Annalise.

"What can Noel do?" answered his mother.

"Call our lawyer. Get someone here right now to clear this up," said Aunt Eleanor.

"Definitely call your lawyer and ask him or her to meet us at the station," Grant replied.

"No, you'll have to wait here for him. No one will be going to any police station."

"I'm sorry but Ms. Sutherland is required to comply with our request."

"Is she under arrest?" Grant turned to Noel, the man was distraught and aggressive with his concern.

"She can be, but we'd prefer not to take that step right now. It's better for everyone if Ms. Sutherland comes with us and your attorney meets her at the station. Since we've been notified that an attorney is requested, we cannot legally question her until that attorney is present."

"But what questions can you possibly have for Annalise?"

"I'm sorry but I can't give specifics."

"I'm coming too!" declared Noel and Annalise clutched at his arm.

"You have every right to do so but you won't be able to join Ms. Sutherland and her lawyer in the interview."

"Why not? I'm her fiancé!"

"And she's an adult. Sorry, but we're leaving now. Do you want to get your purse and a coat Ms. Sutherland?"

Eventually Annalise, tearful and trembling, was put in the car along with the two police, followed by Noel and reassurances from the older women.

When Noel told Judith about it afterwards she could see that he was still upset.

"It's just so wrong that anyone could even imagine that my sweet Annalise would ever harm anyone," he'd said.

It wasn't the type of neighbourhood where lace curtains would be twitching but everyone in the family knew that word would get around soon enough.

Chapter Forty

News that Annalise Sutherland was at the police station rapidly spread through the school. There weren't very many in attendance, but word got out and the answering machine kept filling up with messages from parents – and other people – wanting to know what was going on. Judith erased the lot and headed back to the principal's office to phone Pat Johnson. She wanted to keep the principal up-to-date.

Mark Johnson answered Judith's call and agreed that he was screening his wife's calls but knew she'd want to take this one.

"Oh Judith. I couldn't have chosen a worse time to get sick," complained Pat.

"I'm quite sure you didn't choose it at all!" laughed Judith. "Listen, don't worry about it. We're good at this end. None of us believe this about Annalise, well except for Marta Smith and her crowd, so–"

"What's this about Marta Smith?" interrupted Pat sharply.

"Well, I was told that she's the one who pushed the three students into reporting a scene they witnessed and overheard between Annalise and Noel about Holly, plus Marta also witnessed an incident between Holly and Annalise. It's because of those statements that the police feel Annalise needs to provide some answers."

"I've just about had it up to here with Marta Smith. What is the matter with the woman? She used to be nice – a good teacher and a good person, too – but she's changed."

"Well despite the witness statements the lead detective told me he doesn't believe Annalise had the opportunity or the means to commit the crime."

"So why was she taken in?"

"The higher-ups insisted and he couldn't continue arguing with his boss. I guess they want to show that the wealthy aren't being treated differently. Except that of course they are."

"Oh Lord. That family are our greatest benefactors and Noel is one of our favourite teachers. This is a sorry mess."

"It is, but it will be cleared up. I'm quite sure Annalise has been provided with a top-notch legal team and her interview will be short and professional."

"There is that to be thankful for. Other than this how is everything else going?"

Judith has no intention of burdening the sick woman with Beth's disappearance, so she breezily replied: "Some gripes and grumbles – only to be expected – but otherwise surprisingly smooth. You've got some good teachers who are happy to pitch in and Lila Morelli is a big help as well. We're all managing fine."

"I'm so glad you're there, Judith, although I am sorry about you missing out on your time off."

"Not to worry, I mean look at the weather! I'll take my vacation later on. Meanwhile, I've kept you on the phone long enough. I don't want Mark mad at me! So don't fret, we need you rested and well for start-up in January. Take care, Pat!"

"Bye, and thanks again!"

Lila had come into the office partway through the conversation. When Judith ended the call Lila said:

"So how is Principal Johnson doing?"

"Her voice sounded weak, not like her usual self at all, but flu does hit hard."

"That's for sure, and she's getting on in years, too. Meanwhile, good news: Annalise has been released by the police."

"Already? That's wonderful! how did you hear?"

"Marta is telling everyone. I guess she's been subject to some backlash about how the school folk should be sticking together and not being police informants.

Well, that had to hurt her ego. I've only known the woman for what, three months? but I know that type and being popular and one-of-the-crowd is very important. So, she's been calling the police station all morning demanding news. Finally someone told her about Annalise and she's passing it on as quickly as she can."

"I doubt if she's feeling remorse, but maybe guilty. What do you think?"

"In my professional opinion Marta Smith is a woman who has gone as far as she ever will go in her chosen profession and she resents that fact.

Since there's no longer any chance that she can move up she will cement her existing position by criticizing and stirring up trouble for anyone who has surpassed her. Her habitual nastiness and spite will poison a few of her younger coworkers but because they're young they'll move on and soon she'll have no one left willing to listen to her vitriol. She'll be shunned and lonely, and she should be.

At the moment I suspect she's revelling in all the attention and being 'in the know' so she'll milk her news for all it's worth. Ignore her."

"Great diagnosis. I can tell you've had some experience in the mental health field as well as treating schoolgirls for sniffles."

Lila stuck her tongue out and Judith laughed saying:

"Oh very mature."

"I'm literally back in Middle School so what do you expect?"

"Anyhow, I deleted a bunch of 'what's going on?' messages left on the machine but I'll ask Marta to answer the calls. You and I can send out an email and text update about Annalise. Also, we need to remind everyone that the school is closed tomorrow."

"Are you going to be here?"

"Yes, for the morning. I want to make sure no students get dropped off and are locked out. It's too cold for the girls to be left outside."

"Well then we'll have plenty of time to get ready for Noel's party."

"I forgot about the party. Do you think it's still on?"

"For sure! They'll want to parade Annalise to show she's a free woman."

"That sounds a bit tacky."

"It will also be a great opportunity to get their complaints about the police publicly aired."

"As to that, well I think the police did jump the gun. So to speak! I mean, they did have to question Annalise after Marta pulled her little stunt but I'm sure it could have been done in her home, or rather the Frampton home, instead of at the police station."

"They were making a public show. God knows why. Did I ever mention that I come from a family of cops?"

"No, you didn't. Your dad's a policeman?"

"Actually he's the only one who isn't! well, and Mama of course. No, it's all of his brothers and even his sister, plus his dad – my grandfather – was, and his brothers too. And now my brother, who is twelve years younger than me, is joining the Academy. Real family affair."

"So what does your father do for a living?"

"He's a carpenter. He discovered in high-school Shop class that he loves working with wood so after school he trained as an apprentice and eventually became self-employed. He has a real knack for it and really enjoys his job. It was a good choice for him but it caused a rift for a time in the family."

"I guess in a big family that would be a problem."

"Family support really does matter. In fact, that's why we should go to Noel's party so we can show our support of Annalise."

"You're right YOU should go but I have no interest."

"Oh, come on, let's hobnob with the great and good of Edgemont."

"Why on earth would we want to do that?"

"To poke fun and feel superior!" replied Lila with a smile. "In fact, the stores are open late tonight so let's go buy new outfits to wear!"

"I'm not going anywhere near a store or a mall on December 23rd, thank you very much! and I wouldn't buy a new dress for this anyhow."

"Do you have a party dress?" Seeing the look on Judith's face Lila was quick to say: "Because I've got lots and you can borrow something."

Judith felt a twinge of something emotional, she couldn't identify the feeling, but it made her smile back at Lila.

"That's very kind of you but I won't be attending, I don't want to go. But you go and be sure to tell me all about it."

"I wouldn't miss this party for anything! Now, let's get to work on the next round of updates for the parents."

"You get started, I'm going to organize everyone into the library for another Christmas movie."

Chapter Forty-One

As Judith left the office she saw Brian Penner, Beth's father, coming in the front door. The man looked like he had aged twenty years in the past couple of days. His face was white, his eyes were red, and his gaze was unfocussed. It looked like he hadn't slept since discovering his daughter had disappeared.

He was clearly suffering a terrible ordeal and Judith's heart went out to him. She took his arm and drew him back into the principal's office. Lila jumped into professional mode and got him seated, felt his forehead, and listened to his pulse.

"I'll be right back with a hot drink," she said.

Judith sat down on the love-seat and taking Brian's hand asked:

"What have the police told you? and what are they doing to find Beth?"

Brian sounded completely dispirited as he replied:

"Nothing. They don't have any news and I don't believe they're taking this seriously. They refuse to admit she's been kidnapped. Instead, they talk about runaways and hiding out to get my attention, teach me a lesson, something stupid. They don't know Bethany! She would never, ever do something like that."

He turned a pleading face to Judith as though willing her to understand and agree.

"When I heard they arrested somebody I thought we'd find out where Bethany was but the police said this person has been released! I don't know why they let him go. I don't know if they even bothered to ask about Bethany."

"I'm going to call George Grant, he's the lead detective on Holly's case—"

"That's the problem," interrupted Brian. "They're only working on Holly's case and they don't give a damn about Bethany. They refuse to put two and two together to figure it out. They act like there is no 'Bethany case' but there should be."

His voice rose on a shout and Judith was relieved to see Lila hurry back in the room bearing a steaming mug.

"Drink this – don't argue, just drink," she insisted, helping the man hold the drink to his lips. He made a face exclaiming:

"Ugh, I never take sugar!"

But Lila pushed the mug back to his mouth saying: "You need it, you're in shock. When's the last time you ate? or slept? Don't bother answering it's easy enough to see by your face. Finish this up first."

"I was just telling Mr. Penner that I'm going to call Detective Grant to find out what's being done about Beth."

"Call me Brian."

"Thank you. I'm Judith, and this is Lila our school nurse. Now, give me a minute and I'll make that call."

Judith was glad to get through to Grant right away. Brian Penner was barely keeping it together and she was very worried about him. It was obvious he'd forgotten having met with her and Lila before.

"Grant, hello it's Judith Taylor with Brian Penner, Beth's father. We're wondering how the search for her is coming along?"

Judith schooled her face into showing no expression which was good because Grant told her there was no search. They'd been told Beth had turned up at a friend's house claiming she and her Dad had had a fight and she didn't want to go home yet, she was still upset about it.

"That's a lot to take in. Who told you this?"

"Told them what? What's happening?" cried Brian.

Judith lifted her hand to stop Brian for a moment while she listened to Grant's answer. She asked a couple more questions then said a quick 'thank you' and hung up. Turning to Brian she again took hold of his hand and said:

"Someone phoned into the station saying Beth has been staying with their daughter at their home. She's fine but upset with you because of some fight the two of you had?"

"Wh-what? That's not true! This isn't right. Who was it who phoned saying this?"

"They think it was a man and he wouldn't give his name–"

"They THINK it was a man?" His ashen face quickly turned red as anger took hold.

"The voice sounded like it might be disguised. This voice claimed to be the father of a girl who is also a student here. He said both his daughter and Beth pleaded with him to let her stay another day or so to get over things. He was also adamant that he didn't want to be identified. So they weren't suspicious about his trying to disguise his voice."

"They should have been!"

"I couldn't agree more. The efforts of the police in this enquiry have been distinctly underwhelming."

"It's not right, you know. There was no fight, no argument. I'd hardly seen Bethany in the days before she vanished. This man has got her! how stupid are the police? Why did they believe him?"

"Because he knew about Beth having Holly's diary and being upset over something she read in it. Now, none of us knew about the diary until Beth left a phone message here. That's when we went to your house looking for her. The police had no reason to doubt him. They believed Beth was upset and hiding out and this father didn't want you finding out who or where he is."

"Judith that doesn't sound right to me," put in Lila.

"No, it isn't right. From an outsider's viewpoint the police have been very lax to accept this phone call as a solution. Mr. Penner, Brian, I strongly suggest you go back to the police station and convince them to take your concerns seriously. I can't leave the school—"

"I can," said Lila. "And it's best if I drive, Brian. We won't leave until we've lit a fire under somebody's butt."

The distraught man straightened up and grasped Lila's hand in thanks. He was almost out the door before he turned around to say 'thank you' to Judith as well.

Once he and Lila were gone, she phoned Grant back to give him a heads-up about the forthcoming visit. She didn't mince her words when giving her opinion.

Chapter Forty-Two

Judith decided the Beth situation qualified for a telephone tree. Pat Johnson had given her the password to Samira's computer, and she found the file right on the desktop.

Before clicking the phone links of the six parents who would start the rounds of calling their six who would then call their six, etc... she composed what she was going to say writing:

"Hi, it's Judith Taylor for Edgemont School. I have a few important items so please spread the word.

One, Beth Penner has been missing for a couple of days. We urgently need to find her so anyone who knows anything must get in touch with the police. Beth was Holly Lezinsky's best friend and is very upset about Holly's death. She's only fourteen.

Second item, the school is closed tomorrow December 24th and won't re-open until January 2nd. No students should come here tomorrow, we're not open.

Final item, rumours have been circulating about Annalise Sutherland, the fiancé of our teacher Noel Larkin, being questioned by the police but she is back at home now. It was a misunderstanding and there are no charges. Can you repeat that back to me? and do you think it's clear enough to easily understand?"

She made her six calls and waited for the telephone tree to do its job. If it's true that Beth was staying at the house of a school parent she would be flushed out. Everyone would know the seriousness of the situation now.

Judith was ready for a coffee and a ten-minute break. She went to the staff room but on entering heard Xiao speaking in his quick, high voice, arguing with someone. His back was to the door, and Judith spotted Tanya trying to shush him when she saw Judith. She gave a shoulder shrug of apology.

Xiao whirled round and paused for a moment before confronting Judith about an anonymous letter left in the staff room.

"So, I'm embarrassed that you walked in on that but I'm not sorry about what I said, what I am saying. This anonymous letter makes accusations and we're entitled to an answer." He was belligerent and blushing but unapologetic.

"What anonymous letter? I can't answer you without knowing what's going on."

"This!" he thrust a sheet at her. She'd expected to see words cut-out from a newspaper but the missive was printed by a computer, an easier way to disguise the sender. It was a short message and she read it out loud:

"Judith Taylor and Holly were lovers. Holly wanted out but Taylor wouldn't let her go. Beth knew."

The words didn't register for a moment and when they did sink in Judith couldn't prevent a bark of laughter escaping her lips.

"This is the most ridiculous, utterly ridiculous thing I've ever seen!" she exclaimed.

"That's what you say," jeered Xiao. "But you just denying it isn't good enough."

"It's good enough for me," asserted Eddie.

"Me too," chimed in Tanya.

"Well, I say there's no smoke without fire," announced Marta, her voice carrying over the others' conversations. "You owe us an explanation."

"I owe you nothing," hissed Judith, whirling round to confront her. Marta pulled back in the face of the younger woman's anger but Judith wasn't finished:

"You keep your nasty suspicions to yourself or I will prosecute you for defamation of character. You've been poking your nose into everyone else's business but I will not tolerate you interfering in mine. Do you understand?"

Marta turned to Xiao, expecting him to defend her but before he could utter a word Judith shouted:

"I SAID DO YOU UNDERSTAND? ANSWER ME!"

"Yes, I'm not deaf. You don't have to shout. Xiao was only saying—"

"I'm not talking about Xiao, I'm talking about you spreading gossip and innuendo, egging on the younger teachers, and even involving the students. I demand to know what everyone knows or has heard about this accusation and this filthy poison pen letter."

Everyone denied knowledge of the rumour or the letter.

"Is the accusation true?" questioned Xiao.

Judith was taken aback that he – or anyone – could even think that of her, but her voice was calm and quiet as she replied:

"I'm sorry you feel the need to even ask."

The other teachers looked at Xiao and shook their heads but he lifted his chin and wouldn't meet anyone's eyes. Judith looked down at the piece of paper in her hands, pleased to see they weren't shaking as sometimes happened when she got angry.

"What does he mean when he says 'Beth knew'? Shouldn't it be 'Beth knows'? Does it mean..."

"I don't think you should read too much into that phrasing," said Tanya. "If the accusation in the letter isn't true and of course it isn't! then it follows that no part of the letter is true. See what I mean?"

"I definitely don't believe the accusation," Eddie declared, and there were some murmurs of agreement.

"I'd better keep this," Judith said.

"Don't think you can destroy it, we've all seen it and read it. We all know about it," cried Marta shrilly.

"Why don't I take a photocopy of it for you, Marta? In fact, come with me now, I want to make a copy for the police anyhow."

Judith acknowledged Tanya and Eddie with a nod then left the room without a word, not caring if Marta followed her or not.

Chapter Forty-Three

Judith's mouth trembled and she felt her throat closing but she pressed her lips tight and held her head high. She would not give in to the unaccustomed and unwelcome tears that threatened.

She was shocked by the poison pen letter and devastated when Xiao asked if there as any truth to the accusation. Did he really think she was capable of that and was he the only one? or would many people have no trouble believing the ugly rumour?

First of all, it was inconceivable that she would have an affair with a young student and secondly there was the awful implication that she'd harmed – in fact killed – the girl rather than let her go.

Absolutely ridiculous! but would people, some people, find it plausible? Would the police? Look what happened to Annalise Sutherland because of malicious gossip and all the talk that resulted.

How could she continue to work at the school, a place she loved and where she felt completely comfortable, if she had to live under the weight of her coworkers' condemnation? She couldn't bear to walk into a room where everyone went silent and turned their backs to her.

And what of the parents? would they exert pressure on Pat Johnson to get rid of Judith? She couldn't stand the thought of people whispering about her while exchanging knowing glances with each other.

"Oh, what do I care what they think?" she told herself. "I don't actually like any of these people. If I never saw any of them again it wouldn't matter to me in the least. But it isn't the idea of their poor and misinformed opinion of me that's the problem – it's the utter unfairness of it all. That's what's so frustrating. I've done nothing wrong."

Judith wasn't used to feeling helpless. She regulated and planned all the aspects of her life in order to be in control because being in control had always been very important to her. She'd long ago figured out that was because she'd been forced to take on a custodial role while still very young.

Those times when her mother couldn't take care of her Judith had managed to get by. Her hands and face weren't clean and her clothes weren't washed often enough but she'd gotten herself to school every day. The mess left in the house was always waiting for her and she always came back. Although she'd only been a child somehow she'd coped.

Now, she was struggling with despondency – even despair. At the moment there didn't seem to be a way forward.

She'd been too distant, too unrelatable and cold-hearted. She could identify her failings as a human being but realized she'd never thought they were faults. These traits kept her safe from the hurt the world could – and did – inflict on the unwary and the unknowing. She had learned that lesson at the age of six.

Since then, she'd seen strength in her lack of emotion. No feelings equalled no drama and that meant she could feel superior, except she wasn't feeling very superior now.

"Judith!" she told herself sternly, "Nobody's going to fix this for you so you better hurry up and figure things out for yourself. First of all, what exactly is the problem? Huh! where to begin... someone's made a nasty accusation against me. It's not true but how do you prove a negative? Okay so problem number one is who wrote the letter?

Next problem is why would anyone say something like that about me? am I supposed to be some kind of a threat or something? Is that possible? But why would anyone feel... oh, Holly's killer might think Beth has told me something incriminating.

Or could it have something to do with what's written in the diary or what the killer is afraid might be written there? But I haven't been able to connect with Beth, she's hiding or... or worse.

That other day when I was leaving school I noticed Beth's backpack looked full yet it shouldn't have been since there wouldn't be any homework so close to the holidays. She must have had the diary and some other things of Holly's.

Why didn't I pick her up and drive her home? I might have been able to help her, and there's a chance that together we could have discovered the solution to Holly's murder. Why was I in such a rush? it's not like I have any reason to hurry home."

Yet Judith knew that wasn't the answer. The truth was she hadn't wanted to get involved with a mess of emotions, she wanted to remain at a safe distance.

"And look where that's gotten you," she thought sourly.

"Am I responsible for what's happened to Beth? If she's killed will that be my fault?" Judith was sick at the thought. The guilt was overwhelming and for several long moments she was paralyzed by it. Finally she straightened her shoulders and said:

"Well, enough of that. I need to keep trying to figure out what's going on. So far I need to solve the puzzle of why the letter was written and who wrote it. I can't control whether or not someone thinks I have inside knowledge about Holly that threatens them. No... but I can be alert to that idea and keep my eyes and ears open.

And finally what has this letter accomplished? Can I figure out its purpose? Oh, if only there was someone to confront but who? That's why anonymous letters are so poisonous!"

Chapter Forty-Four

Snow had started falling when Lila arrived back at the school. Judith could see her in the vestibule wiping her feet on the mat, shaking out her hair, and brushing flakes off her jacket. Brian Penner wasn't with her. As she came forward Lila explained:

"Brian is still at the police station. He's determined to see action taken in the hunt for Beth and won't leave until the cops start looking for her. He's very convincing, I totally believe Beth is missing and not hiding. Let's hope he can convince the police, too. Anyhow, that's sorted for... hey, what's up? you look like you've seen a ghost!"

In reply Judith handed over the anonymous letter. Lila read it, looked up in wide-eyed surprise, read it again and made to crumple up the paper but Judith stopped her saying:

"No, I need to give this to the police."

"This is awful, disgusting, despicable, and when we find out who wrote this... this THING well, just let me get my hands on them!" threatened Lila. "But honey, listen, you can't let this get to you. No one could believe this and–"

"As a matter of fact there are teachers in the staff-room right now who asked me if it's true, and Marta's saying, 'no smoke without fire' so it seems that some people do believe it."

"They don't count. They're nothing people, you can't give them serious consideration."

"But I have to!" cried Judith. "Those are exactly the people who will spread it around. Sure, they don't matter to me but this... this garbage does because it can hurt my reputation!"

"Not with anyone who knows you – it's laughable. But–" she put her hand up to stop Judith's protest, "I can see how it's affecting you so we'll figure this out together and fix it. Okay?"

"Well, I have to do something. I plan to give this to Grant and let him investigate because it's obvious this has got something to do with Holly and her murder."

"Before you call him let's get the facts straight. First off, where did you get this?"

Judith told Lila about going into the staff-room and being confronted with the letter but didn't know who found it or at what time. Lila said:

"Let's go find out."

The two women were walking down the hallway when the staff-room door opened on Marta and Xiao. She turned her head away, snubbing Judith, and Xiao followed suit. Lila gave an unladylike snort and said:

"I'll be sure to let Principal Johnson know how well you two protect the good name of the school."

The teachers refused to rise to the bait, which disappointed Lila since she was spoiling for a fight.

Inside the staff-room they found Eddie and Tanya, joined by Jennifer, discussing the letter.

"We're trying to figure out when it was left here. We all agree it wasn't here when we put away our outdoor things and that was by 9:00 am."

"Actually, I was late getting in this morning so I can say for sure it wasn't here at 9:22 by that clock, and it's right," added Tanya.

"Did you have trouble starting your car again?" asked Eddie. Tanya shook her head and smiled saying:

"No, I had trouble starting me! I didn't want to get out of bed this morning."

"So the letter," began Lila, bringing the conversation back on topic. "Can you be sure you would have noticed it?"

"Oh yes!" they all agreed. Jennifer explained that the teachers had all brought in some Christmas goodies to share: home-baked cookies, candies, chips and roasted nuts. Everyone's offering was added to the table and free for anyone to nibble on during the day. When they came in at the lunch-hour all the plates had been pushed to one side and the letter laid out in the cleared space.

"So, the letter was placed on the table at some time between, roughly, nine-thirty to noon?"

"Yes, thereabouts."

"Uh, no actually," disagreed Eddie. "I came in for a snack and a coffee about quarter to eleven. I didn't sleep so well last night either," he added, smiling at Tanya. The women all exchanged a look, for a moment enjoying the budding romance that was going on. It was a pleasant respite from the poison pen letter.

"Actually, that's great, Eddie. It means we can really narrow down the time frame. You were in here for how long?"

"No more than fifteen minutes," he answered.

"Okay so we're talking about roughly a one-hour window for someone to set out the letter and leave."

"If they left," said Lila.

"Oh! who did discover the letter?"

"Several of us came in together. Joanna agreed to take the kids outside for a bit of fresh air before herding them to the lunchroom for hot chocolate. That left the rest of us free to come as a group. We met Marta and Xiao in the corridor."

"They were coming to the staff-room and not from it, right?" clarified Lila.

"Yes, definitely."

"Right, so the actual discovery of the letter hasn't provided any clues but who could have had the opportunity to deliver it?" questioned Judith. "You three were together, with Joanna, this morning."

"Except for the time I was here."

"Oh Eddie, no one suspects you of writing a poison pen!" chided Tanya.

"But we need to look at all absences, even bathroom breaks, because it wouldn't take long for someone to nip in here and set it out."

"But the risk of being seen!"

"Oh that's a good point. The letter writer, we'll assume the writer is also the person who left it here, has to be someone no one would query if they were found in the school."

"And in the staff-room."

"So a teacher, admin, or the janitor. I'm quite sure we can rule out the students," said Judith.

"But a parent could explain their presence saying they were looking for a teacher, right?"

"True. Still, it does narrow it down because the most likely person is a teacher."

"And the most likely teacher is..." Lila didn't get to finish her comment because at that moment a student burst through the door with tears and a bloody chin after taking a fall outside.

Joanna came hurrying in after her and spotting Lila was relieved to hand the crying child over to her care.

Judith thanked the teachers then turned to leave but they pressed her to join them in a snack.

"But I didn't contribute anything," she protested but her objection was waved away by Tanya saying:

"We've got plenty already. Sit down and try a couple of things. I made this, it's a mini-marshmallow chocolate-coated yule log that's sweet and quite tasty despite the irregular shape!"

Judith suddenly felt emotional and had to look away when her eyes brightened with tears. The others pretended not to notice while she regained her composure.

Chapter Forty-Five

After enjoying a relaxing chat with the teachers, everyone careful to avoid the topic of the letter, Judith excused herself with thanks for the Christmas treats.

She planned to go back to the principal's office to make copies of the letter and phone Grant. Instead, she found herself grabbing her coat and heading outside thinking a bit of fresh air would help clear her thoughts.

"I can't explain why anyone would do this to me with one exception... but that's something that makes no sense whatsoever." She strode to the edge of the woods and began walking the perimeter of the lawn. Absentmindedly she pulled up her hood to cover her hair from the falling snow. The flakes were fluffy and soft and the temperature was mild even without sunshine.

"What is the purpose of the letter?" she asked herself and answered: "To throw suspicion on me. But why? any investigation will prove it's all a fabrication. Ah, but what is the immediate result of this letter? Well, it focuses attention on me and away from Annalise. Who would want to do that – besides Annalise herself? The answer to that is Noel but Noel is my friend, or at least a friendly acquaintance, and has been for several years.

Why would he want to do this to me? Oh. What if he doesn't want to but might find it expedient in the short run. After all, the big party is tomorrow night. Him wanting to divert suspicion from Annalise makes sense. He could even mention the letter about me being something laughable – as laughable as imagining the possibility that Annalise could be involved. Sounds pretty convoluted but who knows? It's an idea."

As Judith continued her walk her path was marked by her footprints in the snow but they wouldn't last as the flakes were falling steadily. Her thoughts turned to Noel, and to Noel and Holly, and she wondered.

The two of them had spent a lot of time together working on the play. It was possible – even likely – that Holly had developed a crush on the handsome young teacher. She was pretty girl with a flirtatious manner which would please and flatter Noel. She'd already considered him a likely candidate for the 'girlfriend experience'. Could things have gone too far?

Despite being the victim of a false accusation herself, Judith had no trouble believing the gossip about Noel and Holly.

"And that's odd," she thought, "Since I never linked Noel and Holly in my mind before."

She strode along, unconsciously hurrying as her thoughts quickened.

"Did Noel accuse me of the very thing that he's guilty of committing? He would have no trouble printing out the letter on his computer at home and bringing it to the staff room. No one would think twice if they met him there, he'd simply say "Merry Christmas" or confirm the person was coming to his party. So, Noel could have reason to write it, plus he does have the means to write it, and to deliver it."

She just couldn't imagine her friend doing such a thing.

"Again, I can't figure out 'why me?' Xiao or Eddie would be far more likely. Eddie himself recently said something about the importance of a teacher's reputation, especially a male teacher in an all-girls school. Yes, that's very apropos. Choosing a man to accuse makes more sense so there must be a specific reason why I was named."

The rhythm and pace of her walk stimulated Judith's thought processes and she was able to put everything else out of her mind to concentrate.

"The reason I have to be discredited is because of the phone message Beth left on the answering machine. I commented to myself at the time what bad luck it was that so many people heard it. Noel was one of them. And Noel could have been the intruder in the library. He knows his way around that room and also the hallway for a quick escape.

In fact, the night I left the school and was accosted by Billy MacNeill I felt like I was being watched. At first I put it down to imagination and then to Billy but what it someone else was lurking in the shadows? Lurking! listen to me, so melodramatic! But it is a possibility.

And then there was the guy who dinged my car on the icy road. I put that incident down to bad driving but that car did follow me, mimicking my movements, for quite a ways before hitting me. I was lucky that there must have been a dry patch on that bit of road by the school's driveway, otherwise I could have crashed into one of these big old trees."

As Judith reasoned out her thoughts it did seem possible that Noel was behind the attacks against her.

"But I can't see him as a killer!" she exclaimed. "Although Annalise is biased she was right when she called him a gentle and sensitive man. I can believe him falling into an affair but I can't believe in him committing murder. However, what would happen to Noel if the truth about his affair with Holly came out? I'll think of the worst-case scenario for each consequence:

Number one is that Annalise would break off her engagement so he'd lose a very pretty fiancée and her wealthy, powerful family would make him persona non grata in Edgemont.

Two, would be that Eleanor might cut him out of her will and ostracize him from her social circle. It's only natural that Audrey would stand by her son but their lavish lifestyle is entirely dependent on Eleanor who owns the estate and has all the money. I remember Pat Johnson telling me years ago that Audrey Larkin lived off her sister's goodwill.

Then three would be Noel losing his part-time teaching job. He doesn't need the job which sure doesn't pay enough to support him, but he loves teaching. This job is something he really enjoys doing. But he wouldn't get hired on anywhere else. No school wants a teacher who can't keep his hands off the students.

The final point is the most important because losing his fiancée, home, and job means nothing compared to being jailed for statutory rape.

So, wow, he sure does have a strong motive for silencing Holly and Beth, too, if she knows about their liaison. Especially if she has written proof in Holly's diary.

Where is Beth? I hope the police listen to Brian Penner and pull out all the stops to find her.

She thought about Noel so insistent on driving her and Lila to Beth's home. No wonder he wanted to find her before Judith had a chance to notify the police about the tearful and worried message Beth had left behind.

"And giving in to Noel's urgency got me in trouble with Grant. Suzanne tried to make out that I was playing Nancy Drew or some such thing. She made sure she got her digs in."

Thinking of Suzanne – and Grant – was a distraction. Judith felt she was close to figuring out something important about the case. She now believed she'd let Beth down and felt terrible about that.

"Why didn't I talk to her, or let her talk to me? How hard would it have been to listen to a girl who was so unhappy? Even if it was, as I suspected, just a need to express her grief – why was I so selfish?"

Judith felt that, to an extent, she could excuse herself because of her own upbringing. No one had been willing to help her out – but maybe she'd never asked? and just because she'd developed a thick skin didn't mean every young girl could.

Thinking those thoughts wasn't pleasant but Judith forced herself to face up to her responsibility for what happened and for what she could do going forward.

"I need to stop pretending I can keep everybody at arms-length when the truth is I've been involved all along. It doesn't matter if that's not my choice, not when it is the reality. I can't sidestep the burden, I need to fix this, and I can!"

Chapter Forty-Six

Lila had finished bandaging the injured child and was on the phone asking the girl's mother if someone could come by and pick her up early. Judith only heard one side of the conversation and was impressed by the nurse's crisp, yet reassuring, manner.

"No, as I said no stitches are required and there won't be a scar," she winked at the girl who gave a tremulous smile back. "Yes but she's a very healthy and active girl so these scrapes and bruises are only to be expected. However, she does need some of the TLC that only Mom can provide." The girl nodded.

"I'm glad to hear that and we'll be waiting at the front door. How long do you think? That soon? Wonderful, see you then."

She took the girl's hand saying:

"Lucky you! Mom is going to drop everything and hurry right over. She'll be here inside of ten minutes so let's go get all your gear – remember the school is closing until January so you don't want to leave anything behind.

You will have worn a coat today, what about a hat? boots? mittens in the pocket of your coat? There's no homework – phew – but are you taking any books home to read over the holidays?"

As the girl answered each of Lila's questions Judith noticed that her colour improved. She looked less weepy and more alert.

The three of them headed out of the nurse's office and Lila made the girl laugh when she asked about 'any muddy, stinky gym clothes that need to go home for a wash?' They gathered up the girl's belongings and had her buttoned into her coat and wearing her mittens just as her mother's

191

car pulled up to the school's front door. Lila went out for a quick word then came back in shivering.

"You look the picture of health with your bright eyes and rosy cheeks," she told Judith. "A big improvement since I last saw you, what have you been doing?"

"I've been tramping around the yard getting my thoughts in order and I've come to a decision."

"Do tell."

"I want us to go to Noel's birthday-Christmas party. If, no when, the story of this poison pen letter makes the rounds I don't want it to look like I'm hiding. The party is the perfect opportunity to show that I've got nothing to hide."

Lila clapped her hands in delight, teasing Judith by saying:

"Oh if only Grant could see you now with your high colour and your challenging words. He'd be smitten!"

"First of all that's a silly thing to say and secondly I wouldn't want him to feel that way. I like him but I don't know if we could ever be friends. Friendly, yes, but that's it."

"Suzanne will be relieved, but I'd like to shake you! Not that I believe a word you're saying."

'Oh Lila, you're such a kidder. I do have to phone Grant to tell him about the letter, I meant to do it earlier. I expect Marta has beaten me to it!"

Lila went back to tidy up her office while Judith went to the secretary's office to make her photocopies and then into Pat Johnson's office for some privacy to phone.

She hadn't shared her real reason for attending the party and that was to search for Beth. Judith was certain that Noel had the girl hidden somewhere on the estate. Judith resolved to find her.

Chapter Forty-Seven

Judith got Grant's voicemail, as usual, and left a message saying she had something to show him. He called back right away to say he would stop by in an hour or so.

Judith used that time to get the few remaining students and teachers settled in the library with today's movie. In fact, they would be watching two animations, 'Charlie Brown's Christmas' and 'How the Grinch Stole Christmas'. Judith remembered seeing – and very much enjoying – both of them on TV when she was a kid. She decided to join the audience until Grant got there and sent a text telling him to come to the library.

In the following hour they saw all of the Charlie Brown and half of the Grinch. Judith found that time to be a much-needed break from the emotional upheavals of the day. She was able to relax, chuckle, and hum along to the familiar tunes.

When she saw Grant in the doorway she almost regretted calling him but knew it was best to get this over with. For an hour she'd managed to put the poison pen letter and all of the nasty, suspicious thoughts that stemmed from it right out of her mind.

"It feels like I'm intruding," said Grant by way of greeting. Judith smiled and said 'not at all'. She led the way to the principal's office where the original letter and a couple of copies were on the desk.

Grant read the short letter silently but when he looked up she saw anger in his narrowed eyes and tightened mouth.

"What's the meaning of this?"

"We've all been puzzling over that question. It was left in the staff room between 11:00 and 12:00, all of the teachers who are in today arrived and discovered it together, and it's been handled by everyone. We were thinking it's likely the author is a teacher or a parent. Not a student."

"What is it with you?" he demanded.

"What do you mean?"

"What are you doing to draw attention to yourself? You've become the focus of this investigation." Judith, stung by Grant's comment, gaped at him.

"That's not fair! I'm not doing anything."

"Well it's obvious you've done something! Something has gotten this letter-writer worked up. Something you've said or done has made you a target of his and this is the result," he argued.

"Oh really? That's how you see this? I get criticized if I don't pass on information and then I get criticized when I do. 'Memo to self: don't bother Grant anymore, he'll only get mad at you.'"

"Judith I'm not mad."

"No? well I am. I'm giving you this letter and if you don't think it's important feel free to throw it out. I don't care. Investigate or not, I don't care."

"Oh all of a sudden you don't care. You've stirred things up plenty with Brian Penner, we're gonna end up arresting the guy if he doesn't stop harassing us."

"He should harass you. His young daughter has been missing for days and first your sidekick Suzanne cancels the search because it involved me and then all of you have covered up her mistake by pretending to believe Beth is hiding. No girl hides away from her home and family days before Christmas. She shops and socializes and spends hours on the phone. Your actions, or rather lack of, are a disgrace!"

Lila chose that moment to walk into the office to see the two of them squared off against each other with angry expressions, their harsh words vibrating in the air.

"Uh-oh, I'll come back."

Judith said: "Don't bother, we're done!" At the same time Grant said:

"Never mind, I'm leaving," and went with the anonymous letter crumpled in his hand.

"That was some quarrel, I could hear you right down the hall," commented Lila. Judith was drumming her fingers on the desk and counting under her breath:

"One, two, three, four. One, two, three, four." As a calming technique it seemed to work. She finally looked Lila in the eye and said:

"He's insufferably arrogant and I hate him."

Lila smiled.

Chapter Forty-Eight

"Never mind smirking at me," said Judith. "I'm desperate for a distraction and you've got beans to spill so come on, tell me what's going on with your marriage."

"Sure, I see. You want to feel better by making me feel worse, is that it?"

"Oh no, I don't want to pry if it's painful."

Lila laughed and said: "I'm teasing you. Actually, talking it out with someone impartial might be a good idea. With Christmas so close I've been feeling a bit maudlin and second-guessing my choices so... let's move to the comfy seating and you can tell me what you think. Okay, here goes:

I've been married to Arnie for a long time. We were high-school sweethearts who married after graduation. He got a job with the City of Toronto and supported me while I studied Nursing. I got a good job in a big hospital and our lives were progressing according to plan except we both wanted children and I wasn't getting pregnant. Neither of us had physical problems but there was an issue and that was Arnie's marijuana consumption. It wasn't legal then so he couldn't tell the doctor. I looked into it and although there's been some controversy the majority of studies show repeated use causes a decrease in sperm count and a less motility meaning less capable of fertilizing the egg. But simple solution, right? Arnie just needed to stop toking. Except he wouldn't.

He complained that when I worked nights he got bored on his own. Shift-work is normal for nursing, plus I was doing a lot of overtime due to shortages and, of course, for the money in order to build up a nest-egg. I meant to cut back to part-time once we started our family so a rainy-day fund was a good idea. It seemed to me that this was Arnie's fault for being selfish.

However, I had a good friend who was raising two girls on her own and one time she told me that she didn't blame her husband for leaving. They were very young when they'd married and he wasn't ready to have kids right away. But she pushed it because she was ready and wanted her own home and family. It was her forcing a family on him that ended the marriage.

She was a hard worker, a good saver, and she went on to buy a townhouse and raise those girls by herself because that's what she wanted out of life. Some years later, once he'd matured, he tried to come back because by then he did want to settle down and have a relationship with his daughters, but it was too late. There was no place for him in their lives and no desire to create one.

So, I thought okay I'll back off for now. We're both young and healthy and we've got time. I'm Italian so I had to fend off the constant nagging from my Nonna, wait I've got to do the accents here, okay 'drink some wine and get sexy with him', and enquiries from my Dad asking 'is he shooting blanks, or what?' Mama always said: 'relax and it will happen when it happens'. Family dinners, weddings, and especially christenings were a nightmare. I got to the point whenever someone asked, I'd say, 'don't ask me ask God' and that always shut them up for a bit.

One good thing was that Arnie's family didn't put any pressure on us at all. They're a brainy, academic bunch and he doesn't fit in with the rest of them. Their expectations were low, they'd kind of written him off, and were satisfied he had a steady job with a good income. I get along fine with them but we've never been close.

Life went on with me working plenty – which I loved, I'm not complaining – and Arnie acting like he was still eighteen: getting high, watching tv and playing video games into the wee hours, and talking sports with his buds. My time off was spent cooking, cleaning, doing laundry, and grocery shopping while Arnie looked after the yard, the cars, minor household repairs and maintenance. We always kept busy and we were happy, but we could have been happier.

I know people say it's a mistake to think a baby will solve a couple's marital problems but I really believe having a family of our own would draw us closer together. Not having a family was our only problem. At least it was in the beginning.

Eventually I felt a rift between us. At first I thought he'd met somebody else. God knows he had enough free time on his own and could have fallen into a relationship. I thought that's why I felt him drawing away.

As I mentioned before I'm Italian so I wasn't going to let something like that slide. I confronted him and he was shocked. He said he hadn't even looked at another woman since we got together in ninth grade. I totally believed his denials. But he wouldn't tell me what was wrong. I quizzed him about work and about his health and even about his family. 'Nothing's the matter' he'd keep telling me.

But things got worse. He began having bad dreams and started drinking heavily in addition to smoking a lot of pot."

"Sorry to interrupt but what about his job if he was doing drugs so much?"

"Yeah, about that. Ha. Once marijuana became legal his union managed to stop the City from drug testing. Said it wasn't fair because weed can stay in your system for like a month or something and what people legally did on their off time was their business."

"Oh that's too bad because if it had meant losing his job he might have stopped."

"I think he definitely would have stopped. He likes his job a lot which, believe it or not, is driving a garbage truck!"

"He's a garbage collector? and he likes doing that?"

"Loves it. Ever since they added those mechanical arms to the trucks to pick up the blue and black and green bins he doesn't need a helper and gets to work by himself, He only sees his boss at the start and end of day – if then! He's on his own, out early in the morning, listening to his tunes and, no doubt, smoking all day, enjoying his job.

Anyhow, things between us got even worse. I couldn't stop probing and he just kept shutting me out and finally shutting me up.

I know something is wrong but I can't help him if he won't open up. He says I can't help anyways because nothing's the matter. So we lived in this stalemate situation for awhile longer and then I told him I was leaving. I thought the threat of separation would force him into confiding but it didn't and I can't live with a man who doesn't trust me."

"Oh surely it's not that he doesn't trust you–"

"What else can it be? Unless his secret is something so terrible that he refuses to acknowledge it. Has he done something that he's buried deep down? hoping it will go away? What is he – an ostrich?"

"Ostriches can fight."

"What?"

"Oh that Margaret Sealy, she's doing a report for her Natural Sciences class about ostriches and told me all about them. Far more than I ever wanted to know actually but that's Margaret. Anyhow, go on."

"Not much more to tell. When I decided we should separate I realized I couldn't be accessible. If Arnie really wants me he's going to have to make an effort to come and get me.

And I knew I couldn't stay separated if I didn't get away from all the familiar places and faces. I checked out a bunch of jobs in the National Nursing Registry and saw this advertised. It's completely different from what I'm used to and the money is the pits but it does offer small-town living and a fresh start so here I am."

"What did your parents say?"

"They told me I'm crazy and to hurry back home when I come to my senses. They're okay so long as I'm not talking divorce. But, it's been a few months already – actually since August so like four months – and Arnie hasn't come knocking.

When Principal Johnson hired me I told her I would commit to one year and we could discuss renewing or terminating in the summer. I'm starting to think that it's possible I won't be a married lady by this time next year and I'm not sure how that makes me feel. You see, Arnie and I have been together forever. I have to admit that he's the only man I've ever been with.

So, that's my story. I hope it's been sufficiently distracting?"

"Yes, very much so. You've given me lots to think about," said Judith, obviously going over in her mind everything she'd just heard.

"Good, now let's go check the answering machine one last time and then clear everybody out of here. I'm going to sort through my closet and choose outfits for each of us to wear tomorrow. Since you don't drink you can be the designated driver and pick me up. The thing starts at 4:00 in the afternoon, right? We don't want to be the first people there do we?"

"No, we want to show up when the party's in full swing with a good crowd."

"Okay, so come by my place whenever and we'll get dressed up and go in your car. Does that sound okay?"

"Sounds great. Yesterday wasn't a great day and today has been worse so you're right, it's time to finish up and get out of here."

Chapter Forty-Nine

It was snowing on the morning of December 24th and the air was crisp and cold. Once again Judith appreciated the underground parking in her building. It was comfortable and time-saving to get into a warm car that didn't need to have snow brushed away or ice scraped off.

Of course you never felt the weather was really like until you got outdoors and there had been times when she'd been unpleasantly surprised by the depth of snow on the roads, or the bitter cold of a windy, winter day.

She only saw two or three cars on her way to the school. Most businesses were closed, or closing at noon, today. She was glad today's drive was uneventful.

Judith parked in the no-idling zone to block any cars coming in. Half-an-hour should be enough time to make sure no students got dropped off for a school day. She thought about running inside to check the answering machine but decided no, the school was closed and she would keep it that way. She'd brought her Kindle so was happily occupied reading her book, "Finders Keepers" by Stephen King. She was really enjoying this series.

When the car cooled off enough for Judith to notice the cold she felt she'd waited long enough. Thankfully, No one had come by. Starting the car and setting the heater on high she headed to the grocery store to restock her perishables. She figured the store would be packed and it was.

Despite the crowds and the sense of urgency she felt in the shoppers around her Judith found herself enjoying the bustle as she hummed along to the piped-in Christmas music and wished the cashier a "Merry Christmas".

By the time she got her groceries home and put away, had lunch, and put some make-up on it would be time to head over to Lila's. Judith wondered what outfits her friend would choose for them to wear to Noel's party and was ready to argue if the choice was 'too Lila' and 'not enough Judith'. She realized she'd have time for a nap and set her alarm accordingly.

Lila was living in the basement suite of an older bungalow and Judith had no trouble finding the place when she arrived a few hours later. She parked out front at the curb and Lila met her there before leading the way to her entrance at the back.

"I have a a great arrangement here," she said as she took Judith down a flight of stairs to an open plan living space. "My landlady, she's an old dear, lives on the main floor. She can't manage the stairs which means no one ever comes down here. She has an apartment-sized washer and dryer unit upstairs and I have use of the full-size appliances, including a freezer, downstairs. And plenty of space and privacy. I also get the whole garage since she no longer runs a car. The rent is laughable after Toronto prices, and when I shovel the paths and sidewalk she cooks for me."

Looking around Judith commented on it being cozy and colourful and not what she imagined a basement apartment to look like.

"Oh I'm sure there are plenty of damp, dark, and dingy places but not in Mrs Piernitsky's home. She's Polish or Ukrainian or something and has very definite 'Old Country' values. She keeps the place spick-and-span.

Mrs. P. is a widow who never had kids but there are nieces and nephews and their children who've visited several times since I've been here. She cooks huge meals for them and always passes on platefuls of leftovers to me.

Now, I think I've made a good choice for you to wear but come and try it on to be sure. Judith followed Lila into her bedroom where a dress was laid out on the bed.

"Here's what I'm wearing," said Lila, pointing to a party dress on a hanger with a pair of matching strappy shoes placed beneath it. The outfit looked pretty but Judith was pleased to see a more modest dress waiting for her.

"I'll slip into this and check that it fits me okay, but it looks great." She got into the dress and when Lila spun her fingers, motioning for Judith to turn around, the hem of the dress twirled. It flattered Judith's figure without being the least bit provocative and she was delighted.

The process of dressing up and styling each other's hair was a new and fun experience for her, and she was excited to be going to the party.

Chapter Fifty

The invitation to Noel's combined birthday and Christmas party is always styled as an 'Open House' with people coming in and out all afternoon, evening, and night. Since it's Christmas Eve no one stays too long or too late.

It's a huge social event in the community and is attended by oilmen, ranchers, philanthropists, University presidents, and corporate bigwigs. All the school staff are invited.

Buffet tables laden with festive foods are replenished frequently, and mulled wine, hot toddies, and spiked eggnog flow freely. It's always well-attended and highly anticipated.

Judith and Lila arrived to see the older crowd leaving as the noise levels rose with the vocal enjoyment of happy party-goers.

Judith was going to drop Lila off at the front door since she wasn't wearing boots but they discovered a valet service ready to park the car. They hurried inside and offloaded their coats in the front entrance. They'd timed if right for the party was in full swing, just as Judith had hoped.

Lila had streaked her blonde hair with pink to match the rose-pink spaghetti-strapped dress she wore. She'd found a more conservative style for Judith, rightly guessing that her friend wouldn't wear anything too low-cut or too short. The dress was sleeveless but had a fitted bodice and full skirt that was feminine and flirty. The deep gold fabric flattered her dark colouring. They blended well with the celebratory crowd.

Lila immediately began introducing herself to strangers and was soon surrounded by a laughing group of men and women. Judith envied her ease of manner and knew it wasn't something she could imitate. She turned when a voice called her name. It was Suzanne Mirteau. Judith looked past her to see if Grant was there as well.

"He's not here," said Suzanne still snide even at a party.

"I guess you mean Grant? I'm surprised that the police would be invited considering what happened with you and Annalise."

"Ha! the police weren't invited or if they were the invitation was rescinded," smiled Suzanne with a toothy grin. "No, I'm here as a plus-one." At Judith's curious look she explained: "I'm somebody's date. What about you? where's your date?"

"Oh I didn't need one, I got my own invitation." Judith was dismayed at sounding like she was playing Suzanne's game of one-upmanship so she added that all the school staff, teachers and admin, were invited every year.

At that moment a big, jovial man shouldered his way through the crowd towards them carrying two mugs of rum-and-eggnog. He didn't wait for Suzanne to introduce him saying:

"Hi ya, I'm Raj, sounds like Taj as in Taj Mahal."

"Raj Mahal?" as soon as she said it Judith realized he'd set her up for a favourite tag-line.

"Not Taj Mahal but I do sell palaces! I'm with ReMax." He gave Suzanne her drink and offered his to Judith but she politely declined.

Suzanne's presence was unexpected and unwelcome and Judith could feel the woman's eyes on her as she slipped away through the crowd. Judith most definitely did not want a witness or a watcher. She could imagine Suzanne's jeering voice calling her 'Nancy Drew'.

Judith attached herself to a crowd of women who were going upstairs to 'powder their noses'. She knew they'd all snoop a bit into the other rooms. Judith planned to stay behind when they came back downstairs and do a bit of snooping on her own. Upstairs there was a wait for the bathroom and women were milling about in the hallway or waiting their turn in the chairs set out for that purpose.

A young woman was offering soft drinks, coffee or tea and Judith gratefully accept a cup. She wandered away with her cup and saucer in hand, sipping tea and admiring the artwork on the walls. She moved further and further from the crowd but discovered that every closed door she tried to open was locked. Reaching the end of the hallway she returned and tried the doors on the other side but with the same result. Then she spotted Lila eyeing her.

"What are you up to?" her friend enquired.

"Oh I'm looking around and being nosy. I saw you made some new friends and it looks like you're having a good time."

"I did, and I am, and I still want to know what you're doing."

"I told you."

"You're snooping, aren't you?"

"Yes, that's what I said. It's a gorgeous house and I want to see it all."

"You're not snooping, you're investigating!"

"Don't be silly."

"You never had any intention of attending this party and then, all of a sudden, you wanted to come. Why?" demanded Lila.

Judith decided to come clean. "I'm trying to find Beth. I'm sure Noel has got her."

"Noel?! You think it's Noel?"

"No! Yes, yes... well I'm not sure. Listen, Noel is a great guy and a kindhearted man, but the consequences of Holly's pregnancy are huge and scary and life-altering for him."

"But murder? I can't believe he would kill anybody."

"Okay not murder but what about an accident? He's been spoiled all his life and that's made him weak and when weak people are trapped they lash out. What if he killed Holly by accident and everything that's happened since has been to cover that up?"

"But why cover it up? He's an upstanding citizen with a good reputation and from a good family. I'm sure the police would believe him if he told them it was an accident."

"Right, but then everything he wanted to keep hidden would have to come out. He might be charged with accidental death instead of murder but he'd still be charged. He'd still lose Annalise and his job and his reputation and his freedom."

"Oh yes, of course. Whether or not he meant to kill her only lessens his culpability by courtroom standards – not public opinion."

"That's for sure. So, if Noel has been involved since Holly's death do you think he's responsible for Beth's disappearance?"

"I'm certain of it and that's why I, we, are here. We've got to find her, we've got to!"

"Jeez, keep your voice down! You're convince that she's here, in the house?"

"If she is she's well-hidden. What about in the attic? or the cellar?"

"Cellar? That sounds like something out of a Gothic novel. I don't see how she could be hidden here, there are too many people around. Not just the guests but the employees too and the caterers as well."

"I know, and this place is so big it does seem hopeless."

"Well I'm helping you, no argument. And since it is such a big job why don't we call Grant? Not now, we can keep scouting around now, but you need to call him tomorrow and he can see about getting a warrant to search the place."

"I hardly think my suspicions are solid enough for a judge to issue a warrant on the Frampton estate – especially on Christmas Day!"

"That's not your concern. Go ahead and tell Grant everything you know and suspect. You convinced me about Noel and both you and Brian convinced me about Beth. Let Grant figure out what he can do."

"Grant won't do anything because he thinks I'm a nosy meddler playing detective. We don't need him. He's already told me to butt out and stop interfering so that's fine, I won't pester him anymore."

"He meant that he doesn't want you to get hurt, he's concerned for your safety."

"And I'm concerned for Beth's safety. Tomorrow is Christmas Day, nothing's going to happen, and then it's Boxing Day so again he won't be able to do anything even if he is willing to try."

Another group of ladies arrived at the landing so Judith and Lila excused themselves and got through them. As they made their way downstairs they could see more hallways branching off each leading to many more rooms. Lila spied an open French door leading outside and suggested they leave the hot, noisy room for some air. Judith followed keeping an eye on the pink dress as Lila manoeuvred her way through the crowd.

They stepped outside into a snow-covered world of silence and immediately relaxed. Snow was still falling and the scene, with lighted windows behind and snow-draped trees in front, was picturesque. Looking down to ground-level they saw several smokers standing around indulging in cigarettes and cigars. A pathway led away from the house past garages and other outbuildings.

Judith made up her mind that after they left the party and she dropped Lila off at her home she would come back on her own and explore that pathway from the other end. She was afraid that Beth couldn't wait much longer.

Chapter Fifty-One

Lila was having such a good time Judith suggested she should stay at the party and get a lift home from one of the teachers or call a cab. Lila said no, she'd stick to their original plan. If she stayed any longer she'd end up drinking too much and she certainly didn't want to do that.

"Besides, these sexy-as-hell shoes are absolutely killing me."

"They do look fantastic."

"I know, and they make my legs look great too, but there's always a price to pay and in my case it's pinched toes!"

They laughed together then made their way through the crowd, which had thinned considerably, to find their host and hostesses to say goodbye. They spotted Noel first, with Annalise close by his side, and wishing him a Happy Birthday thanked him for a great party.

"You can't go yet!" cried Noel.

"It's been a blast, truly," answered Lila, "but we're a couple of Cinderellas and it's time we left."

"Thank you so much for coming," chimed in Annalise.

"No, thank you for inviting us. Happy Birthday! Merry Christmas! and thanks again," replied Judith moving away. In the front hall a few Queen Anne chairs were grouped on a colourful Persian carpet with hand-painted Chinese screens providing shelter from the drafts whenever the door opened. Audrey Larkin and Eleanor Frampton were seated here, accepting the congratulations, thanks, and goodbyes of their guests.

"It's so nice to see you two again," said Eleanor.

"You too! and thank you so much for a lovely Christmas party – so festive with wonderful food, a great crowd, and lots of fun."

"We do try," preened Audrey, "So glad you enjoyed it."

"We did, very much! Thanks again and Merry Christmas to you both."

They were led away to find their coats and then out the door to describe Judith's car to the valet. They only waited a couple of minutes and then were on their way back to Lila's, admiring the many houses with Christmas lights and lawn displays that they passed.

"I can't even think about food but I can offer you a cup of coffee," said Lila.

Judith yawned in response and Lila laughed saying,

"You need a coffee to manage the drive home! and then it's definitely an early night for both of us. But I did enjoy myself."

"So did I!" said Judith, surprising both of them.

"You're a fun date, Judith Taylor!"

"Ha! You're not so bad yourself, Lila Morelli."

"I know. You've already got your own clothes in the car, right?"

"Yes, I put them in the trunk when we left your place."

"The richest neighbourhood for miles around and you were afraid of having the car broken into over a bag of used clothes?"

"Hey, fancy neighbourhoods have the richest pickings. Nobody's going to rob a slum."

"You're definitely belt-and-braces, aren't you Judith?"

"I don't see anything wrong with that."

"Not wrong exactly but... does anybody ever call you Judy?"

"Only once."

Chapter Fifty-Two

When they reached Lila's place she directed Judith to a garage in the lane-way that ran behind the property. She had a fob to open the garage door on her key-chain and Judith parked in the empty space beside Lila's car. To get in the house they only had a short walk along a bricked path across the backyard to Lila's private entrance.

"Feel free to have wander around or if you're tired just take a seat. Coffee will take two minutes. I've got Vanilla Hazelnut if you like flavoured coffee, or else regular medium roast coffee, your choice."

"I wouldn't mind trying that flavoured coffee if it's not too much trouble."

"It's no trouble at all, I just pop in a pod." When Judith looked quizzical Lila showed her the single-serve coffee maker. It sat beside a huge stainless-steel machine which Lila explained made wonderful espresso and cappuccino with frothed milk but she wasn't firing up the contraption tonight. "It takes so long to get it going that I feel obligated to have several cups and I'm just too tired. I don't know if it was the drinks or the cold air when we came out but I'm ready to crash."

"Oh don't bother with the coffee then–" began Judith but Lila interrupted saying:

"Too late! it's already made, see?"

They took their mugs over to the couch and Lila flipped a switch on her stereo system and Christmas music began to play.

"Won't your Mrs. P. object to the noise?"

"No, the old sweetheart is deaf as a post once she takes her hearing aids out which happens about 8:30 each night."

Judith sipped at her hot drink and felt comfortable and relaxed. She needed to kill some time before sneaking back to the Frampton home and the coffee would help her stay awake. \\

Lila, having kicked off her high-heels when they walked in the door, now massaged her feet and sighed with pleasure.

"Despite everything else that's been going on this evening I've found myself thinking about your marriage, well, your separation. It's surprising. You seem very upbeat but it can't be an easy situation for you. If I'm being intrusive just say so, I'm not trying to poke my nose in."

"You're funny, Judith. To answer your second question no, I don't mind you asking. As for the first question well, yes and no. Being so far away from everyone I can forget about my 'Toronto problems', for awhile anyhow. Tomorrow is going to be tricky. Arnie and I have celebrated every Christmas together for almost twenty years, I mentioned we started dating in high-school, right?"

"Yes, that's a long time."

"I'm kinda thinking this holiday will be the catalyst, I guess, for what comes next in our married life."

"You don't strike me as the kind of person who just sits back and takes what life throws at you. I mean, you've mentioned your Italian temperament and Arnie, well with a name like Morelli he must be Italian too so—"

"No, Arnie's not Italian, he's a Canadian with British ancestry. Morelli is my maiden name. I figured if I'm making a new start I don't want to be making explanations over name changes or stuff like that. If I stay here I'm Lila Morelli, if I end up going back to my married life no one here will realize I was using my maiden name all along.

I don't know if I'm being practical or practising for life on my own. I've never been on my own, actually. I went from my parent's home to my home with Arnie. This is the very first time and I have to admit I quite like it."

"I've pretty much always been on my own. I'm an orphan. Dad died when I was a little kid and my mother passed a few months before I finished high-school."

"Oh that must have been devastating!" exclaimed Lila.

"Well, no," after a brief pause she continued saying: "The Vice-Principal at the school had me stay with her and her family till the end of the semester. They were very kind. I lived in the dorm at University and that was almost like living alone because I rarely saw my roommate. She was the 'party hearty' type. Her expression, not mine."

"And she didn't manage to convert you?"

"Ha-ha. I know you're kidding but funny enough we stayed roommates all the way through because our differences meant we suited each other. Since we had minimal contact we didn't have the falling out issues or raiding each other's wardrobes or stealing boyfriends problems that I would hear other roommates fight about.

Halfway through my last year she dropped out to get married and they didn't assign me another roommate so it all worked out great for me."

Lila was giving her a funny look but when Judith said: "What?" Lila just shook her head saying,

"Well I'm one to talk, I've only ever had the one boyfriend. Only one man has ever seen me naked and that's hard to believe at my age and especially in this day and age. I've seen more nudity on TV then I have in real life and I'm a nurse!

Arnie and I have been best friends since we were young and we never really formed other close relationships. He has buddies from work, as did I, plus I've got a ton of cousins and plenty of young aunts, too. I've always had female companionship to go out for a meal or to gossip with but not a close girlfriend. Oh boy..." she interrupted herself with a jaw-cracking yawn. Judith laughed and gathered up her things saying,

"I can see you do need your bed so I'll be on my way."

"I'm being a crappy hostess but I'm not going to argue. I really am beat. Just leave that mug. I'll zap the garage door and after you back out jut give a quick honk so I can zap it shut again."

They walked up the stairs and Lila opened the door and pointed her fob. Judith heard the garage door open and said goodnight. Lila thanked her for the ride and she thanked Lila for accompanying her to her first-ever Noel Larkin birthday-Christmas party.

"Maybe the first of many, who knows?" replied Lila before closing the door against the cold night air.

She stayed there looking out through the small window. Judith backed out and gave her horn a beep then waited while the garage door closed before entering the back lane and heading home.

Chapter Fifty-Three

Judith studied the map on her computer, zooming in to the Executive Estate subdivision. She was pleased to see that, as she suspected, there was a service road leading around the back of the big properties.

It was a proper-sized road, big enough for garbage and recycling pick-up as well as delivery vans.

Judith followed the line to the boundary of the Frampton home. She planned to pull her car over under a cover of trees and then slip down the lane entering the property from the rear, as unobtrusively as possible. She already felt self-conscious, silly even, in her all-black outfit and switched her phone to airplane mode now before she forgot.

Leaving one lamp on in her living-room and careful to be quiet Judith left her apartment. There was some sort of get-together going on downstairs and guests had blocked the driveway, forcing her to leave her car on the street. She'd been annoyed about that when she got home but now realized this was a good thing. She was able to leave as anonymously as any visitor.

Driving back the same route she'd taken hours earlier Judith felt a thrill of excitement. For such a non-adventurous person she sure was having her share of intrigue tonight.

There was very little traffic. The still-falling snow was melting when it reached the road but piling up to transform the shape of hedges and gates and even parked cars. As she neared the Estate she again admired its Christmas card type of scenery.

Finding the service road, she slowed down since it was unlit although the driveways into the properties had lights or fancy lanterns to outline the way. She found the Frampton place and driving her car a little further along the road she pulled over onto the verge and parked.

It was pitch dark and utterly silent. Walking back Judith felt the first frisson of fear. She couldn't distinguish the ground from the driveway, the snow lay thick everywhere, but she kept moving in the direction of the house even though she couldn't see it yet.

It was so quiet. She strained her ears to pick up any noise but couldn't hear a thing, the falling snow deadened all sound. If she'd been walking here with a friend it would have been pretty, but on her own it felt a little creepy.

Judith had an aha! moment when she spotted a small building, like a cottage. She'd remembered Noel once talking about their guest house and how it was great in the summer but not much good in the winter since it wasn't heated.

"There is a wood-burning fireplace," he'd said, "but that only lasts for an hour or so, it won't keep you warm all night." He'd gone on to describe what a cozy little place it was hidden away in the woods and Judith had thought it sounded like a rich man's love-nest.

She recalled that conversation now as she crept closer. "The guest house looks deserted," she thought. "It's dark and there's no smoke coming from the chimney."

Cautiously looking around Judith noticed her footprints following behind her. Looking ahead she saw a fainter, smaller set – almost filled up with flakes – leading into the woods. "Beth!" she thought and followed the trail.

Tree roots snagged underfoot and thorny branches stabbed at her. Despite moving with as little noise as possible Judith knew she'd been heard when a gasp and a tearful hiccup sounded about a yard or so in front. The woods were too dense to let in much light from the moon, so Judith was relying on her other senses to direct her.

"Beth it's me, Ms. Taylor, Judith Taylor. I've come to take you home," she called in a loud whisper.

"Ms. T-Taylor?" quavered a young voice.

"Yes, yes! I'm so glad you're okay. You are okay, aren't you?"

"I will be now that you're here. I've been so scared. I don't know how long I've been in that cabin but I finally got up the nerve to break a window and climb out. I'm sorry about breaking the window, though. I feel really cold but I was cold inside there too."

"Well, I'll crank up the heat to high once we get in my car and you'll soon warm up. Oh, I'm so happy to find you! your father's been half-crazy with worry."

"Dad! Oh, I've missed him so much. I want to go home! Let's go right away."

The girl stepped out from behind the tree where she'd been hiding. She wasn't dressed for a December night outdoors and was visibly shivering. Judith hurried forwards and put her arm around Beth's shoulders. She immediately turned it into a hug and Judith could feel the cold of the girl's thin body right through her own outdoor clothing. She slipped her coat off and wrapped Beth in it. Then locking their arms together the two of them started back.

As they reached the edge of the clearing and got closer to the house Judith could see larger footprints coming towards the guest house and overlaying Judith's as the larger prints went around to the back of the small building.

The size of the print and length of the stride indicated a man made them – and he was running. The sight was terrifying.

Judith hesitated, feeling unsure which way to go. She could barely see the lights of the main house which mean it was quite far. The follower might still be at the guest house itself and going deeper into the woods to head for the back road was scary.

What if they got lost? Beth couldn't take too much more exposure. The girl was weak and frightened and bitterly cold. But Judith, indecisive in such an unfamiliar situation, had to make a choice. She felt safer hidden in the confines of the woods although she knew it could be a dangerous route.

"It's time to get rid of 'sensible Judith'," she told herself, "But taking risks sure is scary so I hope my sensible self will return as soon as we're safe and sound."

As quietly as possible they waded through the snow and around the trees. Every now and then Judith's head would brush against a branch releasing a shower of snow. It was dark, it was cold, and they were frightened.

They heard the occasional skitter of some small creature but had no fear left over to worry about it. They knew there was a man nearby and he was tracking them.

Chapter Fifty-Four

The silence and blackness of the woods was unnerving. Judith was glad to have Beth to hang on to but she could feel the young girl's strength running out. She dragged her feet, sometimes threatening to pull them both to the ground as she stumbled and almost fell.

They weren't moving very fast and Judith feared it wouldn't be difficult for their pursuer to catch up. Their only hope was to remain hidden by the trees while he stayed on the path.

Beth cried out when the man suddenly jumped in front of them. Judith's heart started pounding when she saw he was Noel.

"Finally!" he exclaimed. "I've been up and down around here. I was following your footprints but couldn't believe you'd stay in the woods. I don't know if you're brave, crazy, or stupid but I've got you now."

"Let us go!" screamed Judith but Noel grabbed her and covered her mouth.

"Shut up!" he demanded. "There's nobody around to hear you but I don't want to listen to that noise."

He snagged Beth's arm with his other hand and started pulling the two of them back where they'd come from, towards the guest home. Judith kicked her feet then let her body sag inert weighing him down, slowing him down. Noel struggled with her for a bit then flung her away. She fell in the snow in a half-sitting position, the wet seeping into her thigh and hip and side. Her black track suit was no protection and she'd given her coat to Beth.

"You don't want to come with us that's fine," shouted Noel. "You're not the one I want anyhow, she is." And with that he started dragging Beth away.

Judith saw that the girl was too weak and too tired to put up a fight. She let him lead her away.

"Stop Noel! stop right now," Judith hollered but he ignored her and kept going.

She thought of running back to her car to turn on her phone, get help... she wanted to do all that – so much! – and it would be the smart thing to do, but she fought the temptation because she couldn't abandon the girl. Noel had Beth so Judith had no choice but to follow.

Chapter Fifty-Five

Judith reached the guest house shortly after Noel and Beth. She raced inside expecting to find him holding Beth with a knife to her throat or a gun to her head. Instead, she saw Noel striking a match to the logs laid in the fireplace and Beth huddled on the couch with a blanket. Before she could speak, she heard the front door open and a voice complaining:

"Oh Noel, we only lost one, but you've brought back two! Who is this? a teacher? no it's the accountant woman. What is she doing here?"

Audrey Larkin, well-bundled against the cold in a smart coat, fur hat and warm boots, whining about Judith should have been farcical. Instead, Judith was terrified.

Noel's mother had a strong sense of privilege but surely, she understood she couldn't sweep away Noel's crimes of kidnapping, false imprisonment, and murder? Motherly love taken to the nth degree. Unless she was raving mad.

"Mother stop, please. This has gone too far."

"Darling boy, so sweet and sensitive. You've always needed me to take care of you and you always will. And I will always do so. The solution to this problem of yours has been very tricky but I'll figure it out, don't worry.

I thought I'd given this little Miss a strong enough dose. She's very thin so what she drank should have done the job. I can't understand what went wrong."

Judith gasped at the realization that Audrey Larkin wasn't covering up for Noel's criminal acts but for her own.

Beth stared wide-eyed at Audrey, too petrified to move. Both Noel and Judith stepped between the woman and the girl.

As Audrey reached into her purse Judith had to suppress an hysterical laugh at this crazy lady primly carrying her handbag over her arm. The laughter was choked off at the sight of the gun Audrey now held in her hand.

"Step aside, Noel. I need to take care of the girl and do a proper job of it this time."

Shaking his head and giving a deep sigh Noel said: "Oh, Mother you aren't going to shoot Beth, I won't allow it."

He stepped forward to take away the gun, but right then the door banged opened startling Audrey who fired the weapon. The noise was immense. Noel fell to his knees and someone screamed, it sounded like they all screamed.

Eleanor Frampton stood framed in the doorway.

Chapter Fifty-Six

"Audrey! what have you done now?" Eleanor exclaimed, but her sister didn't answer. She had rushed to Noel and was crying over him.

"Mother I'm fine, well it hurts but the bullet only grazed me."

"You're bleeding!" she screeched in horror.

"It's only my ear, you know ears bleed a lot. Honest, it's okay, I'm okay."

Keeping her eyes on Noel and the women Judith edged towards the couch unnoticed. She sat down and pulled Beth tight against her. The girl buried her face in Judith's shoulder and her whole body heaved with sobs. She was terrified.

The other three forgot about them as they squabbled about why Audrey had a gun and where she's gotten it:

"I took it from Bas's office right after he died. You never missed it."

"I never knew he had it."

"Well, I knew. I saw it lots of time when I was in there just... looking around."

"Snooping, stealing, prying – up to no good as usual," Eleanor retorted.

"Well never mind that now. Noel needs to go to the hospital and I have to get rid of this girl. Oh, and I guess this woman too."

"What are you talking about? Noel, what is your mother going on about now?"

"God knows, Auntie. I don't. At the party I saw Judith poking around like she was looking for something then I realized it was someone that she was looking for. It had to be Beth. But I knew Beth wasn't in our house because she'd gone into hiding or something and then, I don't know why, but I thought of the guest house. It's a perfect hideaway–"

"That's what I thought too!" said Audrey brightly. Her son and sister stared at her in consternation then Noel continued saying:

"I came out and spotted traces of footprints which shouldn't have been there so I followed them. The door was locked but, as usual, the key was on the door-sill.

When I came in I felt a strong draft and discovered the window was broken. Looking out I could see signs that someone had left here by breaking the glass and falling onto the snow. Other things in this room had been moved about, and a knapsack with Beth's name on it was left behind.

It was unimaginable that Beth was hiding out here by choice, and the broken window told its own story so–"

"She shouldn't have broken anything!" said Audrey with annoyance.

"I went out looking for Beth and followed a trail of two sets of footprints into the woods. I wasted time heading back home, thinking that's where Beth and whoever had gone, but ended up having to double-back. I found them – still in the woods – on their way to the road. I didn't even think about what Judith was planning to do, all I could think was that I wanted to bring Beth back here to get her warm. If she's been locked in here, in the cold, for a few days she must be suffering from exposure. How far were you planning to go?" he asked, turning to Judith.

"My car is on the service road."

"Oh, I should have asked instead of just acting but I wasn't thinking straight. It's a shame though because we three would have been away by now and I wouldn't be bleeding like a stuck pig... Mother you could have killed me!"

"It's obvious that the girl is fine," said Audrey. "I guess she was out cold for most of the time. I thought she'd be dead. It never occurred to me that she'd wake up and escape." She shot Beth an evil look but the girl's face was still hidden and she didn't see it.

"But why? Why did you want to kill this girl? Noel couldn't have gotten her pregnant as well."

"WHAT!" shouted Noel. "I've never gotten anyone pregnant, what are you talking about?"

"Well dear we know about the condition Holly was in when she died–"

"And you thought it was mine? That I got her pregnant? She's a child! And she's a student. I would never have relations with student. How could you ever think something like that of me?" Noel was flabbergasted – and hurt.

A feeling of shame swept over Judith as she realized that because of gossip and innuendo she'd also believed the worst about Noel. She was no better than Xiao and Marta for so readily believing the accusation made about herself in the poison pen letter.

She owed Noel an apology but if he even imagined she had accepted that rumour as true then their friendship would never be the same. She decided not to admit to her thoughts.

"When I see the doctor to get my ear stitched up I'll arrange to give a DNA sample as well. I – God, I can't believe you could possibly think..." he shook his head and a few drops of blood out flew striking his mother in the face.

"She told me so, that's why!" Audrey answered. She looked around at all of them saying:

"You all know she'd been phoning the house for Noel. Well I demanded, as his mother, to know what business she had with him. She said it was a matter best discussed in private. That set off warning bells in my head and I was angry too. This nothing of a girl insinuating something underhand.

So, we arranged a time, and I told her to meet me here in the guest house and when she hung up she said, laughing, 'bye-bye Granny'. I slammed the phone down. Right away I realized her plan was to ruin my son. Well, I knew I could deal with that by buying her off since it was obvious from the type she was that it was money she was after."

"Mother you have no idea what Holly was like. Sure she could be flippant but she was funny and clever and had a future."

"Noel you are so naive! and don't interrupt me. Anyhow, this Holly did turn up but was very late with some excuse about her planned ride not being available, so she'd had to hitchhike and walk a long way. She was very cranky and sassy, and I was annoyed too because of the long wait – it's so cold in here – and next thing I knew she was saying something smart-alecky and I hit her. She fell right there." Audrey pointed to the floor to the side of the fireplace. "I waited for her to get up and when she didn't, I went over and pushed her with my foot. Her body lifted a bit and I saw a big pool of blood. That's when I realized she was dead."

"How could you be sure?" cried Eleanor. "Did you check for a pulse? what if she could have been saved? you should have called 9-1-1!"

"No, no I knew she was dead, and I was glad. I didn't want her resuscitated. It actually worked out well because even though I'd come prepared to pay her I expect she would have kept coming back for more. This way the problem was taken care of once and for all."

"There was no problem!" thundered Noel. "If she was pregnant it certainly wasn't by me!"

"But how could I know that, son? She was very convincing and I'd heard Annalise complain about this girl who was cozying up to you at rehearsals, holding your hand, whispering in your ear, and after all you are a man."

"That's right, Mother. I'm a man, not some predator or child-molester. You killed her for nothing."

"Noel no, don't say that! I killed her for you!"

Audrey's dramatic cry brought Grant, Annalise, and Lila came through the door. They'd been standing outside with Grant holding the women back so he could listen to the conversation, which turned out to be a confession.

Annalise rushed over to Noel and hugged him tight, exclaiming over his injury. Lila ran to Beth and began checking her over, saying:

"I need to get this girl to the hospital right now, she's severely hydrated and running a fever."

She glanced at Noel and frowned at the blood, but he smiled at her over Annalise's shoulder and gave a thumbs up sign.

Eleanor Frampton sat down on a kitchen chair and started to cry. Audrey looked around in surprise saying:

"Don't you want to know how I go the body to the school?"

Chapter Fifty-Seven

Judith might have been very angry with Lila if she had known what her friend was up to but she didn't find out until much later.

Then she learned that Lila's worries stemmed from not being able to reach Judith on the phone. Lila said she'd woken after napping for a few hours feeling refreshed but regretting her poor hostessing. She wanted to make up for it by inviting Judith to have Christmas dinner with her next day.

It wasn't like she'd had a premonition of danger or anything, only a sudden thought that neither of them should spend Christmas alone. She got worried when she couldn't reach Judith even though it was after 11:00 at night. It didn't make sense that Judith wasn't answering.

"I had a very good reason for not answering!" laughed Judith when they did sit down and talk through the events that led up to the confrontation in the cabin.

Lila wanted to go over to Judith's apartment to make sure she was okay but knew she had drunk too much at the party to drive. Although she felt fine and alert her nurse's training taught her that she must still have alcohol in her system. Too much to be out driving.

Thinking about all those peculiar incidents that had befallen Judith over the last few days made up Lila's mind. She called the police station and asked for George Grant, claiming it was an emergency. Lila couldn't care less if she caused trouble – she was deeply worried about her friend.

Again, Judith laughed. It was easy to forgive after the fact.

Lila insisted Grant come get her to accompany him to find Judith. He tried to get her to divulge Judith's suspected whereabouts but Lila was adamant that she wanted to tag along.

They all met up again at Judith's apartment. It was late, the wee hours of the morning in fact, but all three wanted to talk about the night's events and each had a story to tell.

Chapter Fifty-Eight

Grant took a sip of his coffee before starting. He noted that Judith used a French Press and the coffee tasted great. Since his presence wasn't required at the police station and as it was now actually Christmas Day he was on his own time which he mentioned:

"I can now say 'Merry Christmas, Judith and Lila' because it's officially the 25th. Since I don't have a family I usually offer to work over the holidays but this year I think I'll enjoy the break."

"I've worked my share of Christmas and New Year's shifts too. Judith, you're lucky you're in a nine-to-five job."

"You wouldn't know if from this past week – that's for sure! Anyhow, Grant, tell us what happened with Audrey Larkin."

Grant told the two women how Eleanor Frampton had called in some favours and Audrey had been whisked away to a psychiatric facility masquerading as a 'rest home'. Grant's boss had assured him that the woman was under police guard and would be arrested, but Grant suspected the doctors would pronounce Audrey Larkin unfit to plead so the case would be resolved without going to court.

"So they're saying that she's some kind of psycho?"

"Yes, they are. According to Eleanor Audrey suffers from 'one of those pathys' but she couldn't remember if it was psychopathy or sociopathy. She claims Audrey was diagnosed many years ago and the family has always had to keep an eye on her. So long as the afflicted person is never thwarted they never need to act on their latent tendencies."

"I can believe that," put in Lila.

"Well, it all sounds a bit gobbledy-gook to me but I'm only a dumb copper," replied Grant with a smile.

He turned serious and said to Judith:

"Speaking of dumb, I want to apologize for snapping at you yesterday. It happened because of my concern for your welfare, but that's no excuse. The truth is both Lila and I took those near-misses far more seriously than you did. I believed that someone was after you, and I thought it had something to do with Holly's diary."

"Which I never did have."

"But the person chasing after you didn't know that."

"That was Noel," said Judith. "While Lila went to the hospital with Beth, and you were busy with handing over Audrey, Noel and Annalise and I had a good talk. He felt guilty that Holly died because of him and said he couldn't believe what his mother had done.

Annalise and I reassured him that he wasn't to blame for that but then I said, 'your mother didn't come into the school and leave an anonymous letter in the staff room', and he said he was really, really sorry about doing that. Annalise didn't know what we were talking about and when I explained she burst out laughing. Well, it was ridiculous.

Anyhow, her laughter broke the tension and Noel confessed that he was desperate to deflect suspicion from Annalise, her being questioned really upset him. It was touching to witness because he really does care for her. Also, he'd heard some of the whispers about him and Holly, and I think that was an eye-opener for him.

He told me 'I was going to name Marta, because no one likes her very much so it would be believable, but you're the one Beth left the message for on the answering machine' and he apologized again." Judith didn't add that Noel had also said 'besides, you're tough' because she wasn't sure how she felt about him saying that.

"But what about the intruder in the library and your car getting rammed?"

"The intruder was Noel. He was trying to scare me away from my desk so he could search it for Holly's diary. He was worried that Beth had somehow gotten it to me or hidden it for me to find. Noel went too far in his flirtation with Holly but it never went beyond kisses and compliments. He was afraid she might have written a glamourized version of their friendship making out it was something much more. Sounds to me like he's learned his lesson and won't be so susceptible to adolescent hero-worship in future!

You know, I do feel badly for believing the rumours about him. Since Noel is so good-looking and the heir to a huge fortune I guess I assumed he'd be spoilt and have a weak character. I was wrong. He's a nice guy and a good guy and I should have been a better friend. Especially since I know how it feels when people are ready to think the worst of you."

"Nobody believed that letter, Judith. But you're right about Noel, we all made assumptions. Just like people do with blondes, right Grant?"

"Don't go there Lila," he growled.

"Getting back to the incidents, the bad driver following me might simply have been a bad driver but I think it was Audrey. We know she has her own car and could come and go with no one the wiser from the estate."

"Yes, she explained that when she told me how she'd moved Holly's body."

"Tell us about that part. She's a small woman, did she have help?"

"No, she bragged about how clever she'd been. Do you remember seeing a bearskin rug – a real black bearskin – at the side of the fireplace?"

"No," said Lila, while Judith answered:

"Yes, I noticed because it should have been in front of the fireplace and I was admiring the skin. Usually people have a small white rug in fake fur."

"Well, Audrey told me she rolled Holly onto the rug and dragged her to the door. Then she brought her car around and drove it right up the guest house. It has its own gravelled driveway which we couldn't see because of the snow. It must have been a struggle, but she managed to get Holly, still wrapped in the bearskin, into her car.

Then, she said she was exhausted from the effort and took the car back to her own driveway where she left it with a body wrapped in a bearskin rug for several days because she forgot!

She's lucky it was cold but not cold enough to freeze the body once rigor mortis ended otherwise she wouldn't have been able to get it out of the car.

It wasn't until the chauffeur finally asked if she'd like him to move her car into the garage that she remembered Holly's body was still inside. She drove to the woods behind the school, unrolled the body and returned the rug back where is belonged but moved to a different position to cover up the blood stain."

"That wouldn't have worked for long though. The guest house must get cleaned?"

"Not thoroughly, not until the summer when it might be used by visitors."

"But wouldn't the blood stain still be there?"

"Yes, but faded and why would anyone think the stain was blood? And if they did the family would simply have called the police to report a break-in and some sort of incident of which they'd claim they were unaware of.

Without a body we wouldn't take a sample and even if by some chance we did it wouldn't be tested, lab fees are expensive and we have to justify the costs."

"Wait a bit," said Lila. "I know crazy people can sometimes find incredible strength but how did that old lady manage to do everything?"

Grant laughed replying: "You made the same mistake I did, Lila. What makes you think Audrey Larkin is old? She isn't fifty yet!"

"Wow, really? Oh my. I guess it's just her being Noel's mother and not working, sitting around a cozy fire all day with servants taking care of everything while she griped and complained, with her cameo brooch pinned to her cashmere dress... hmm. You're right, I assumed she was much older."

"Well Eleanor Frampton is considerably older and they're sisters so that adds to the assumption, I guess."

"Do you realize," said Judith with a surprised look on her face, "She could very well have gotten away with it!"

"The perfect crime."

Chapter Fifty-Nine

Lila swallowed the bite of shortbread cookie she was eating to say:

"She might have gotten away with killing Holly but then Beth got involved. She told me about that while we waited for her Dad to get to the hospital," Lila turned to Judith saying: "You should have seen his face! he was so happy he cried, and he even gave me a kiss. You should have been there."

"Why? Does Judith want to be kissed by Brian Penner?" asked Grant with a wry smile that didn't quite reach his eyes.

"He is very good-looking, if you like that type..." Judith let the sentence trail away. "I'm sure he considers Beth's return to be the best Christmas present ever."

"Is Beth going to be okay?"

"She'll be fine, Grant. She's a healthy girl and at that age they're able to bounce back. Still, she was at risk and not only from Audrey Larkin! exposure to cold temperatures for a long period of time has adverse effects on the body's organs.

Fortunately there is no frostbite so now we just have to hope she can get out of the hospital without picking up the flu bug. They've got a lot of people there who are sick with it."

"That's another reason why nobody likes hospitals!"

"Anyhow, when Beth couldn't get hold of you, Judith, she tried to reach Noel. See, she'd read Holly's diary. She had no reason to be afraid of Noel because she knew he wasn't the father of Holly's baby."

"Who was?"

"According to the diary Billy MacNeill was the father," said Grant. "Beth turned it over to us and it seems Holly had enjoyed stealing her mother's boyfriend and the two of them acting like they were barely friendly under Dana's watchful eye. Holly had complained a lot about Dana being too strict with her.

I bet Billy MacNeill was the ride who never turned up to drive Holly when she met Audrey at the guest house. Remember? he was in Calgary that day."

"Does that mean he cooked up this scheme to extort money by claiming the baby was Noel's? and Holly was going along with it? I guess she must have been, she's the one who made the phone call."

"They must have figured Noel's mother would pay to hush up a scandal without investigating the matter."

"And they figured correctly. Audrey Larkin just went off on her own to take care of things. I wonder what would have happened if she had asked Noel about it?"

"Holly was pretty brazen. She'd probably have laughed it off telling him that because he was so rich it was worth a try."

"Poor Dana. I know she kicked Billy out after discovering the whole car theft thing but to find out this as well... does she have to find out?"

"Yes, she has the right to know. It will be painful but it's always better to know."

"So, before you hijacked my story I was saying..."

"Sorry, go on Lila."

"Beth called up Noel but, like Holly, got his mother instead. I guess Audrey was feeling invincible after killing Holly and the subsequent disposal of her body, so she arranged to pick up Beth outside the school.

Instead of taking her to the house she told her that the servants were terrible gossips and she'd prefer to have a private chat. When they got to the guest house she poured out hot chocolate from a thermos for both of them. That's the last thing Beth remembers until she woke up feeling sick to her stomach, stiff, and very, very cold."

"The hospital will look for traces of a drug or poison in Beth's bloodstream but it's unlikely that Audrey Larkin will ever be charged with attempted murder," put in Grant.

"So that's it? No one is held to account and we're all supposed to go ahead and get on with our lives like none of this ever happened?" Judith looked intently at Grant and he returned her stare. Lila, feeling out of place, stood up saying:

"I've got to get going, my family will all be calling at the crack of dawn because they always pretend to get the time difference backwards. They'll start off nicey-nice, wishing me a Merry Christmas, and then complain that I'm not there to help cook the big dinner.

Speaking of which Judith just come over whenever you feel like it. I don't have a turkey but I'll make you a nice dinner." She gathered up her coat and purse then remembered she didn't have her car since Grant had picked her up.

"Oh, I'd better call a cab."

"You won't get one on Christmas Eve, actually it's Christmas Day now, isn't it?"

Grant paused a moment then got up as well casually remarking:

"Yes, it's been a long day for all of is, hasn't it? Maybe we can meet up for a drink or a meal or something over the holidays?"

"Maybe," answered Judith.

Chapter Sixty

"Happy New Year, Samira," said Judith, happy to see the secretary over her flu bug and back at her desk.

"Same to you, Judith. I'm sorry we left you in the lurch," she dropped her voice to whisper, "I think Pat's going to tack on another couple of days when you do take your vacation, but don't let on I said so," she added.

Judith winked at her to the amazement of both of them.

Knocking on the partly opened door Judith still wore a smile as she entered the principal's office. She plopped down in the visitor chair announcing:

"I am so glad to be sitting on this side of that desk again. Imagine, it's only been two weeks! Holly's body was found on December 19th and here we are on January 6th, two-and-a-half weeks later, and it's all 'done and dusted' as I've heard people say."

"Judith, I can't thank you enough for everything you've done. I know I said some of this when we talked on the phone but you were wonderful. From having to cancel your vacation, to dealing with school issues and parents and teachers, then the murder and the police, and Beth Penner going missing and then finding Beth!

You know Eleanor Frampton can't say enough about you. I gather you were in the nick of time to prevent a bad situation from becoming very much worse."

"Oh everyone helped in that regard: Noel, Lila, Grant, and Eleanor herself. But to be honest I did get more involved, in fact way more involved, then I thought possible. There's something about these girls that... I don't know – grows on you? There's a strong feeling of responsibility but it's good, it feels right. I'm not making any sense, am I?"

"On the contrary, you are crystal clear. Judith, I can see that this experience has changed you, and for the better. I mean, there was nothing wrong with you before but now you seem happier, more relaxed, or something."

"You're right. I felt okay about myself and my life before but now I feel... great!"

"It shows. I'm so very glad that things turned out the way they did."

Judith left Pat's office deciding to grab a coffee before starting her day's work. As she passed Samira the younger woman looked up and asked:

"Judith have you met someone?"

"Don't you start, I hear enough of that from Lila!"

A few teachers were still in the staff room when Judith walked in and they all exchanged friendly greetings. Even the people she suspected had doubted her before now made friendly overtures, including Xiao. Judith answered questions about the Christmas Eve incident to the satisfaction of everyone except Marta who glowered from the corner.

In the corridor on the way to her own office she called out "Love the new glasses, Margaret!" and "Happy New Year" greetings to the other students she passed. The spirit of community wrapped its warmth around her.

In the privacy of her office Judith opened her purse and once again read the "Happy 2020" New Year's card she'd received from Grant. It made her smile and it felt right, but for now it was her secret so she didn't display it on her desk.

Don't miss out!

Visit the website below and you can sign up to receive emails whenever Della North publishes a new book. There's no charge and no obligation.

https://books2read.com/r/B-A-RNHX-DNMGC

BOOKS 2 READ

Connecting independent readers to independent writers.

Also by Della North

Village of Edgemont
A Deadly December in Edgemont
A Fatal February in Edgemont
A Sinister Spring in Edgemont

Watch for more at dellanorth.ca.

About the Author

Della enjoys mysteries that won't keep her up at night, have a hint of romance, and a satisfactory ending. Preferably in a series.

She and her partner live with a tuxedo cat in the sunniest city in Canada, nestled in the foothills of the Rocky Mountains.

In November of 2022 Della undertook the National Novel Writing challenge to complete a 50.000 word first draft and the Village of Edgemont series began.

Books in this series:

1 - "**A Deadly December in Edgemont**"

2 - "**A Fatal February in Edgemont**"

3 - "**A Sinister Spring in Edgemont**"

A portion of sale proceeds will be donated to NaNoWriMo.org in appreciation.

Read more at dellanorth.ca.

www.ingramcontent.com/pod-product-compliance
Lightning Source LLC
Chambersburg PA
CBHW020058180626
46812CB00006B/2387